Love in the Reality

Love in the Reality

Is not always that easy!

Hardik Dhamija

MAHAVEER PUBLISHERS

Published by
MAHAVEER PUBLISHERS
4764/2A, 23-Ansari Road, Daryaganj
New Delhi – 110002
Ph. : 011 – 66629669–79–89
Fax : 011 – 41563419
e-mail : mahaveerpublishers@gmail.com

First Published: July 2011
Second Impression: September 2011

Love in the Reality
ISBN (10) : 8183520855
ISBN (13) : 9788183520850

Distributed by
VAIBHAV BOOK SERVICE
e-mail : vaibhavbookservice@gmail.com

Distributed in Nepal by
BAJRANGBALI BOOK ENTERPRISES PVT. LTD.
Jyatha Mushyabahal, Ward No. 27, Kathmandu, Nepal
e-mail : bajrangbalibooks@gmail.com

Printed by Jaico Printers, New Delhi

Dedications

Dadaji and Dadiji (Badi Mumma)

Acknowledgement

Thank You God! Guruji!

Thank you! This one is for each and everyone, who has contributed in one way or the other to make it possible. I don't remember the names at the moment but they have done a lot. Yipeee!! It's finally happening.

Great work requires great efforts and efforts can only be put up by great people, so there are many great people, who've contributed in the making of this novel. So, let's start the list – My PARENTS (love you!), my GRANDPARENTS and the three lovely PRINCESSES (my three second to mother.. Sorry! I'm a little mesmerised—my sisters, Charudi, Sakshidi and Guddudi). They all have given their best and I am what I am, just because of them. They all have made my life beautiful. Thank you, the best family in the world.

Life is all about learning, whether from here or from there. Most importantly, the mentors in my life (I know, I can never give back whatever they've given me) – Meera Ma'am (it would have been impossible without you) and Mammaji.

Now, the people, who have supported me all the way, so hats off to them for being so helpful, all my batchmates and seniors, who have heard the story so patiently and some got so involved in the story that they would argue and put their points. Kritika, for being the first reader and making me realise that I can write a novel. The unending list of names of my bastard friends (I expect, at least now they'll read the novel on finding their name in the acknowledgement because most of them have a soft copy of the novel but never thought of reading it once) – all my buddies and friends and seniors, the most enjoyable time in P. U.

To all the girls, who've managed to read and respond nicely, including Sargam.

Support by the following people and their curiosity to read the novel has carried me all the way – Ashadi, Utkarsh, Ashmit.

Special Thanks to all the people, who've criticised my work, which actually provoked me to give my best.

I am very grateful to Mahaveer Publishers, who have turned my dream into a reality and the reality is in your hands. It is they who have worked to get this in your hands—Mr Binay and Mr Dilip, thanks a lot sir! The Editing team (thank you!)

Thanks to all the people in my life, who have loved me and those, who have not, I am longing for your love. Hope this novel is just an effort to bring more love in my life. It's all yours! It's the love of everyone that has invoked me to write and carry this message (in the story) to you. Tidoo and my Jiju, actually I completed this on the day of his birth.

Thank you Bhanudidi for suggesting the title.

A Word or Two

If life took me on the wrong path, I cannot hold it responsible for it because my fault was no less in failing to realise what was right and what was wrong and take the right path, instead of allowing life to drift like a leaf fallen from a tree. I always knew that I was wrong and knowingly exacerbated the situation, because I was deluded by my sexual urge which became another inexcusable reason for my crime. It all boils down to the fact that I was a bloody loser. I even started hating myself and I had ample reasons for that.

You may ask why I started to hate myself.

It indeed was strange that loving the world and knowing that the world loved me and accepted me for what I was, I do not know to this day why I came to hate myself.

I loved myself, when I was free,
But hate myself now when I have grown into a tree.
The chains that kept me bound carried me away,
Now I realise,
I am far behind from where I have to stay.
I reached the pinnacle of success,
but it was not mine.
It may be a wonder for others, but for me, it was happiness for a moment of time.
My dreams were decided by the greed of others,
And my life has become a stretcher dragged by others.
I feel shy in front of Him.
I want to cry in front of Him!

He created me to reach the sky, but I feel pity that I can't even jump to touch Him so high.
The world loves me
And I love the world.
Even then I don't know
Why I hate myself?

This was the first and the last poem ever written by Drishya Roy but I love it Aditya because I have penned down my true feelings on paper and it is all a fact.

"So, how did you propose to her?" I asked him (he was lost somewhere). My curiosity level had reached its zenith and the story was at its climax. I was damn certain that she would have said 'no' and that is why he was still single.

He started again, "It took me three months to muster the courage to confess the sins and wrongs I had committed. Finally on a day of fine weather, I took her out on an evening walk to an old temple, after seeking permission from Shubh. I was shrinking and squirming with fear the entire way because I was afraid that I would lose her once I confessed all the wrongs that I had committed in life. Nevertheless, I was determined to let her know the truth about the person she thought she loved. We sat down on the stairs in front of the temple. I placed my hand over her hand in her lap and bent down my head because I could not face any girl while revealing the dark truths about my past. But like a dam allowed to burst, once I began, I blurted out each and everything, beginning my life story since my childhood and including Rhea, alcohol, drugs, Casanova, brothels, Radhika and finally how I underwent a change after meeting her, how a tizzy feeling surrounded me and how I lived in a state of euphoria, all because of her."

Hardik Dhamija

The past—I was just that way...

October 1, 2009 (22:00 hours)

I had quite a busy life being an engineering student. It was a back-breaking job. Come to think of it, education itself is a burden on each and every student born on this earth because he is always buried under heaps of assignments, scores of projects, dozens of books and what not. Ironically everything seems completely strange; in short, education is only a conglomerate of problems, especially for a student like me, who believes in taking bold and unusual actions. Three years passed in studying for my degree, but even then the greatest idler, that is I, have survived because of my belief in my *ulta dimaag* which has kept me afloat through the most serious of situations and this includes the bloody IIT and AIEEE exams too.

Rock on every beat of life, It is to play and rock and that is what I am doing here, sitting in the centre of the Green City (Chandigarh, Sector-14), enjoying the environs. I do enjoy sleepless nights (night outs, when we spent our nights in the mountains, discovering new ways to reach Kasauli, Shimla, Dharampur and many other unnamed names. There were times when we actually witnessed God's creativity at its peak with the sky divided into two different colours – colours which even our branded cameras could not capture. I felt helpless and useless because despite being an engineering student, I was not capable enough to invent a device that could compete with the human eye. I decided to leave all this for students like Einstein others and concentrate on living in the present, enjoying every breath of air, the firm ground below my feet, the blue sky above because after all, that was what my life was all about. It was not the time to discuss night outs enjoyed during my college days or abuse the creepy education system. It was time to discuss my love, my Aprajita.

Dhan-te-na-tan-tan..............

My cell phone began to ring and it was Aprajita on the line. "Hello madam! Hardy Boy at your service 24 x 7," I said politely.

"Stop joking!" she said angrily.

"I am not...," I began but she interrupted me to ask angrily, "What do you mean by saying at your service 24 x 7?"

"Actually the first time in my entire life...," but again she stopped me midway to shout, "Mr Confucius (Chinese philosopher), stop blabbering."

"My cute little Hindu College girl (because she was pursuing her B. Com. from there), tomorrow my parents-in-law are going to complete the most traumatising 25 years of their life."

"Shut your mouth! It is their 25th wedding anniversary."

"Yeah, that is what I am saying. They have survived even after doing the great wonders."

"What great wonders?" she screamed.

"They created an inimitable beauty with an unpredictable character like you," I explained (that's the greatest problem with girls: they always need a bloody explanation though I concede that girls are really the most interesting characters on earth created by God).

"Are you trying to insult me?" she thundered.

Oh God, another explanation but I took the shortcut. "No! No! I am sorry but tell me, have you prepared for the surprise party to be held for my parents-in-law to be?" I asked (Thank God, I could succeed in changing the topic).

"*Bhaiya* and I have planned to throw a party for them."

"Wait! Is Rahul *Bhaiya* here?" I queried.

"No, he will be here by tomorrow."

"Great, my future *saala* (brother-in-law) is helping a lot. I am impressed. I will gift him a BMW," I said in an excited voice.

"Oh, not again your Bayerische Motoren Werke," she said in a taunting voice.

"Hey! Uncle D has got a new BMW-X9, worth Rs 59 lakhs. I will soon ride it," I said in a proud voice. (I was really proud of Uncle D!)

"Great *yaar*!" she said happily.

"First tell me, is there any preparation required to face the great challenge? AJ, you must tell them about our relationship."

"Hardy, I am really scared," she said in a faint voice.

"Dear AJ! What's the meaning of your name?" I asked between clenched teeth (how could I make her brave enough to confront her parents?)

"Oh shut up! I know it better than you."

"AJ, I know you know it better than me but at times you need to remember that Aprajita means 'the indefatigable', 'the one who can't be beaten by any sort of situation' and that is what my Aprajita should be."

"But, Aditya, I am worried about their reaction."

"*Jaan*, just behave like a warrior and speak out the truth in front of them."

"No, it will not be easy."

"No! It should be a Mickey-Mouse job for you. If you could survive a five-year relationship with me, then why should you be worried about tackling your parents? Just chill, *yaar*," I prodded her. She seemed thoroughly amused. I have noticed that girls enjoy it when boys make fun of themselves and they love to laugh at them. But then, love can make you do anything, even listen to taunts just to see your lover smile.

I continued, "*Bachcha*, if we wish to see our relationship acquire the form of a permanent bond in this impermanent world, then you will have to confront them head on. There is no point in playing hide and seek with them. Look, if you do not tackle the bull by the horns at the earliest, the tension will keep on building up inside. It is better to do today what has to be done tomorrow and why not do it just now rather than keep it stored within till you are able to muster the courage to face them?"

"What is going to happen? I am really scared," she said in a trembling voice.

This is the most irritating situation in love when you have to keep on persuading, cajoling and prodding your loved one to go and reveal your love story. Moreover, since girls are past masters in bursting into tears, which can melt even a stone-hearted person (I hoped her father was not one), I thought she could easily overcome any objections that her parents, especially her father, would raise, by resorting to tears. "Be cool, *yaar*! Do not expect the worse though you can be prepared for the worst, though I feel that everything will be alright in the end," I said in a cheerful voice.

"I think you are right," she said pensively.

I really did not know how to incite her further to tackle her parents though had the task been given to me, I too would have quivered in my shoes. Anyhow I must have sounded convincing because she agreed to tell it all to her parents, possibly my persuasive powers had done wonders. I think it was the magic of love which could turn a normal person into a crazy one, who keeps on blabbering without using the mind.

"Yeah, I always am. You must have seen that all great persons…" but I could not end my sentence because she shouted, "Cut down that crap!" She never allowed me to speak much because she dreaded to listen to any of my high-brow philosophies which I was apt to quote in situations like these.

"Okay madam! By the way, your parents cannot have a better son-in-law than me, that is, if they are a bit intelligent. They should willingly accept me."

"Hardy, that's enough for today," she said imperiously.

"It is not. I again want to let you know that I love you."

"Are you alright?" she said suspiciously, as if I had given her the news of a third World War.

"Yeah, I am! It is just that I'm a bit serious about the issue. So tell your parents as soon as possible about us and invite me for the party tomorrow."

"Obviously you are invited," she shot back.

"That is what I wanted to hear, my Aprajita, who is invariably convinced about whatever she does!" I said, gearing up.

"See you tomorrow *besharam* crook. All is well that…"

"'B…y…e!"

She believed greatly in God and disturbed Him by calling out to Him every time she got into a situation that was beyond her control.

The past—An excerpt from my diary...

Thank God, Rahul *Bhaiya* is coming. Actually the dude had nothing to do with me but invariably managed to emerge like an angel from the most pressing situations in my life. He was three years older than me and a good friend of Shahid (my best friend). They both had worked together on various projects and scored a cup in the State-level Basketball Tournament. Moreover, it was natural for a student like Shahid to be famous among his seniors.

When a human being gets involved in any sort of affair, problems stalk his steps like a shadow, never leaving him alone, even if he is an experienced player. You can find solutions to your problems, but you can never escape the reality, especially when you are caught in love. In a love affair, the sword is always waiting to tear your skin apart. This is more so when you are an inexperienced player (obviously a 15-year old child cannot be expected to tackle such a disaster). You are liable to commit an unavoidable 'mistake' in a situation where life is moving swiftly.

Being a child of just another *Homo sapien*, I committed the mistake just after three months of proposing to her. Like all other idiot lovers, we began to chat through messages, which I was very good in composing because of my *ulta dimaag.* As on any other ordinary day, I messaged her:

"Googly-woogly, your lovely cheeks,
Love-love-love, for what I peek.
Lots of hugs and kisses waiting for you,
You are Aprajita and
I am the beaten one for you."

I used to send her such messages every day and night, but such messages or not, if death knocks on your door you cannot avoid it. God alone knew what made Aprajita's mother check her daughter's phone and read that message (it was not meant for her, but parents are apt to forget their manners when it comes to their children, like it or not. On such occasions, no matter how you try to convince them, nothing works. All your efforts prove futile and like every other parent, they are ready to tear you apart). Her mother told her that she wanted to talk to my parents. It was enough to make me wet my pants. My *ulta dimaag* failed me for the first time in my life.

A true friend is always helpful and comes to your rescue as Shahid did. He took the lead and sorted out the matter with Rahul *Bhaiya* on the condition that I would not see her again. Fortunately, Rahul managed to convince his parents (though I cannot help wondering how anybody on earth could succeed in convincing a Hitler-like Dad, the tall man with a long beard, who always reminded me of being Emperor Aurangzeb's reincarnation. His deadly eyes could even provoke Mike Tyson to shit in his pants and his heavy deadly voice was no less than that of an Army General).

Love is above every fear and our relationship proved it. After Class X, we were together again and as experienced players. Now, we were tired of playing the love game surreptitiously and just wanted to apologise for hiding our relationship and come out in the open. At times, either out of childishness or immaturity, you tend to throw all caution to the wind and do things without caring about the results. Not once, but many a time I have wondered how we managed to survive in our relationship despite all kinds of threats and admonishments waiting at every step. We were threatened with dire consequences if we tried to see each other but distances only strengthened our relationship and made us realise the importance of seeing each other. It was in moments like these that our relationship became special; the moments which made us realise that we were one. The occasions when I felt the earth slipping from below my feet, the time when I escaped my first heart attack in life are still fresh in my mind.

The past—A ridiculous start made a great journey...

March 2003

Who the hell said that schools were meant for learning? A school should be a place for children to enjoy their life without any tension. Studies were not such a torture at a young age as one could easily score 90 per cent marks by being attentive and without being bothered by love affairs. Shahid, Vibhor, Viny, Aman, Pumpi, Rohit, Vishal and I (all great planners) would enter the class with the firm determination to rock the classroom on the basis of our chant, "No studies on the first day" and we would engage the entire class in a chalk-war. So, with our pockets full of chalks stolen from the library (pilfered actually by engaging the librarian in talk) we would turn every idiot in the class into a helpless soldier of chalk-war. When we entered Class IX, we decided to sit down in different corners of the 36 x 12 ft room.

I started the game by calling out to Vishal, "You asshole!" and as soon as he turned to look at me, I aimed a piece of chalk directly at his left cheek (that may have shaken his breath for a second). In retaliation, he tried to hit back but (unintentionally) found another idiot as his target. Finally, one after another, the whole bunch of idiots in the class got involved (obviously not all can be followers of Gandhiji), aiming the chalks at one another and shouting with joy on hitting the target, "Yippie, mission accomplished!"

Like all true creators and inventors, I would be enjoying it all for creating such chaos in the classroom. We did what we wanted and made the idiots do exactly as we wanted. Once, I managed to hit someone really hard and the victim turned out to be the one who was following behind Shahid (though my target was the latter because the thrill of burning the best friend's ass gives the greatest amount of pleasure). The chalk piece flew and landed straight on her face. Crap! Crap! How could I?

In front of me stood a scintillating beauty; no, how could I hit an angel who had landed straight from heaven? Indeed, she was different to any other girl that I had met so far. She was so beautiful that all the monsters stared at her, forgetting all about the chalk-war. Coming to earth, I thought, she had to be some princess from a royal family and I was sordidly tempted to drop to my knees and, like a royal guard, exclaim, "Madam, this is not your palace." But, instead of saying anything, all I could do was to stare at her dumbstruck. I wondered if I could ever talk to her and which language could she be communicating in with commoners like me! She was simply awesome! I felt she could not be from the planet Earth because she was too cute, too charming, too alluring...Oh God! I was lost!

I moved my eyes from her peaches-and-cream complexion, round face with dark brown eyes, long black hair in which I could easily get lost and moist, pink lips. I was tempted to touch them, actually kiss them because they were so tempting. Her nose and a black spot below her lips on the right side caught my attention. As my eyes travelled downwards, I literally flunked. She was wearing our school uniform (I had considered our school dress rather drab and dull) which made her look all the more attractive. My eyes noticed a very perfect body encased in the school uniform (ironically, at that moment, I was envious of that uniform which could have the pleasure of covering the body of the greatest beauty in the universe). Her long legs (I had an overpowering urge to feel them), that were visible below the hem of the uniform looked so silky that I was tempted to run my hands over them. My hands craved to touch her; my eyes could not refrain from staring at her; my brain seemed to have lost all senses; my nose feverishly inhaled the beautiful smell of her fragrance; my heart thudded with full velocity; and my feet seemed ready to collapse. I was completely lost. I felt she was the sea in which I wanted to drown. This was something that had happened for the first time in my life. Yeah, I was completely lost.

But such sweet experiences are not long lasting. I did not know why, but the fact is that you have to accept the bloody reality. While I was busy gaping at the beauty, a piece of chalk came and hit me on my right cheek. As I was caught completely unawares, I screamed with the shock of the pain. The princess turned towards me and I became embarrassed to have caught her attention and that too when I had been the one to hit her. I think I was made to pay the price for hurting a princess.

Suddenly, a voice croaked (I do not know who the bloody hell produced that abominable sound), "Are you a new admission?"

She nodded (damn, she was so beautiful).

"What's your name?"

But before I could get over the shock of seeing such an ineluctable beauty, entered the Hitler with a changed sex and disguised in a dirty green sari to bring order to Class IX. For me, actually, every other teacher was a Hitler, who wanted to rule over this 36 x 12 ft room which they considered their German empire and we, the students, their fucking prisoners, who knew nothing except to swallow the shit emitted from their bloody mouths.

The attendance began and for the first time in my life, I was fully attentive, keen on catching the newcomer's name. My eyes were stuck on her infinite beauty and my ears strained to catch her name. I could not control any of my senses and kept on concentrating on the roll call. Suddenly my ears caught the name 'Aprajita Khanna' and I was completely beaten and lost. Her name, meaning the one who cannot be beaten, had floored me down; why only me, actually every boy in the class. Oh God, what a beauty she was and one who could hypnotise everyone around her. She was a killer, a witch, a thief, a scene-stealer and so beautiful. She had taken everything of mine and like a helpless dog, I kept on gazing at her since the moment she had entered the class.

The past—We boys were totally mad...

Aprajita Khanna had become our new target…

Pumpi, Vibhor, Shahid and I, as also the others, were captivated by her mind-blowing beauty. We usually say girls excel in gossiping but I am sorry to say that when it comes to boys, we are capable of spreading news about girls faster than the speed of light. Due to our extraordinary capability, the buzz spread, among the huffing monsters from Class IX to XII and this included even the juniors, that a new bombshell had joined Class IX and the victims were the boys of our class, who kept surrounding her, trying to talk to her. Unable to extract much information from her lips, they were given to asking each other, "Can she be single?", "Is she studious?", "I have heard about her boyfriend but who is he?" Wanting to attract attention, they tried to spread rumours about her though none knew much about her. Most of the other students were seen wandering around our class, trying to catch a glimpse of her and trying to enter our class on some pretext or other, either to ask for chalk or ask the teacher for explanation of some problem. Being a boy myself, I could understand their situation because like me, I think, they also thought that by taking a look at her, they all could spend the rest of the day by dreaming about the beauty. I enjoyed it all as it gave me the opportunity to interact with all my seniors and juniors, to discuss the hot babes in the class, who could not help remarking how lucky we were to have a classic beauty in our class. But somehow I was not enjoying it because there were some crude and uncouth comments were being made on her personal attributes. They made me feel insecure, possibly because I had started liking her. No, it was not true love. I used to watch other goodlooking girls in other classes, but on seeing the new entrant, I felt that they were all alike while Aprajita was head and shoulders above them all. She had carved a special niche for herself in my heart, though this was not my first time. I had felt the same for many other girls initially as they used to rule over my brain and innocent heart but sooner or later I would realise that it was mere infatuation on my part. I assumed that the same would be the case regarding Aprajita but I found it was true love that I felt for her. May be I had changed because nothing remains constant. I did not know what was happening but I knew I was caught in a whirlpool of emotions, though unwittingly. It was

God's fault for making me a boy who is always considered to be weak in the heart when it comes to the question of girls.

Befriending Aprajita had become the object of attention for every boy in the school, but we, the lucky bastards, had the advantage of having her in our class and our group was not the normal one to go and say "Hello!" We were decent boys and tried to employ decent tactics to win her attention. We subscribed to the philosophy that we were different and we acted different. Our group had its own unique style to attract the new entrant. So the game started on the second day itself with some pre-defined rules that we people had chalked out from the worst part of our brains in Class VI and were still following because we monsters enjoyed and loved to do everything that was out of this world. We were apt to putting up hoardings on the roadside, clicking photographs of couples kissing, spraying abuses and locking the teacher in his or her own house when the Hitlers were asleep or busy in sex with their partners. The objective was one and the same: 'To get the girl'(either through ragging which often left the newcomer completely baffled in the very first month of her schooling or taking candid photographs and embarrassing the girl by clicking her when eating or scratching her head, or getting angry. This time the victim was Aprajita and we licking bastards had the advantage over her as she was one and we were many. We had chalked out certain rules to be followed by every monster and these included:

- Every monster was awarded one week to mix with the girl and no other monster was allowed to be seen around the girl during that week. The guy had the freedom to use any trick or means to impress the girl during this five-day game.

- On a Saturday, the boy had to propose to the girl, regardless of what the girl's feelings were.
- The last conversation between the two had to be repeated word by word in front of all the other monsters.
- The first boy's name was selected on the basis of the age-old tradition of drawing the lots.
- Last and most important rule was that we all had to behave as strangers, so that the girl would not get any inkling of her being a victim of a pre-planned game.

Our motto behind the game was strong determination (to prove our true name, the Monsters) because it took a lot of courage to stand as a shameless guy if caught red-handed. We monsters had often experienced a lot of humiliation, thanks to our cruel teachers, including the *Dian* (Diana), our class-teacher. To fulfil our objective of getting to know the girl, we mad boys believed that any girl could be ours within a week, no matter even if the girl was a Miss World. We believed that we could change the shape of the sun into a square, no matter if science proved it to be on the contrary because we held the belief that 'impossible meant that it was possible'. It required only a different attitude to look at things as a result of which we monsters could go ahead but move in the order of our names – Pumpi, Vibhor, Shahid and Aditya.

The past—Get the girl in a week or...

1. Monster Pumpi

Monster Pumpi or Vikas Aneja was a dude, whose parents possibly forgot his real name with his wet diapers and began to call him Pumpi. He was an extrovert and a sprightly 15-year old dude who knew how to turn the tables in his favour. He lived as if he was on top of the world and addicted to girls. He was always seen with one girl or another. Aprajita was just another target for this addict, who happened to be the best debater in the school and the silly girls were only too eager to hear his words of appreciation. I always wondered how they managed to tolerate him, who kept on bragging about his achievements all the time (he and his mind-boggling experiences could never come to an end).

On the very first day of the week, he managed to find a space in the newcomer's heart by talking about the teachers and the school, besides bragging about his debating ability. Soon he became her guide and her only acquaintance (we all were bound to our own rules) to acquaint her with the various events of the school, the teachers, the students, the labs, the functions, etc. The programme continued for the next four days and the dude played the big shot on Friday when he insisted on making the English teacher take up for discussion the topic 'Female Foeticide'. As expected, he was the first speaker. Being a good speaker, he could hold the audience spellbound with his rhetoric and which would have taken me a thousand years to articulate equally nicely. He began, "Thank God, they did not kill the first woman on Earth; otherwise I would not be present here. We would not be having such beautiful girls in our class (pointing at Aprajita but suddenly turning to Ma'am), including our beautiful teacher" (he knew the art of buttering). Aprajita kept on looking at him for the rest of the speech, with the three of us grumbling, "She is gone! She is gone!" We all were screwed. All I could remember was that everyone clapped excitedly (as if they had been granted 100 per cent scholarship) when he finished with his speech, except for her and us.

Yeah, *Pumpi* was a champ at articulating his thoughts and views and we all felt totally defeated and bereft. At lunch break, he took her out on the lawns for a walk and told her, "You know every girl has a crush on me but I have been floored by the one who is different from the others and that is you. I really like you. I have discovered that I keep thinking about you all day and night. I know we hardly know each other since you joined only a week ago, but I like you and yesterday during the English class, I became a confirmed disciple of you."

She kept on looking at him with a doubtful eye all this time, before uttering, "Are you serious?"

"Yeah, I am," he had replied promptly.

"I do not know, Vikas," she had replied with an effort to avoid him.

"What do you mean by that?" he had asked calmly.

"I had never thought that way," she had said in a low tone.

"So, think over it then!" he had said desperately.

"Is it some kind of a joke?" she had questioned.

"No! I am serious," he had said as if the level of desperation had reached its zenith.

"Vikas, I do respect your emotions and undoubtedly you are an ideal guy whom every girl wants to date but Pumpi, you are not my type. You are great but whenever I think of you, it is as a friend and I am sure a guy like you can be a good friend. You can have any girl as your girlfriend because there are so many sexy babes who would be willing to befriend you."

"So, madam, a handshake to mark a new beginning," (he beamed and I realised that he would not let any opportunity slip without trying to trap a girl).

"So, friends we are!"

"Yeah, friends."

Finally, Pumpi entered the cafeteria and we all kept watching him, waiting to hear the result. He started smiling and that wacky smile made me cry out. We however, desperately wanted to hear the outcome from his mouth.

"She's not my type," he said, still smiling.

"What?" we all squealed together (that's human nature. When you are prepared to lose a match and someone informs you that you have won, idiotic words like "what", "how", "when", are bound to emerge).

"She's too studious," he replied in a low voice, but continued to boast about himself.

Deep in my heart, I felt as if I was in the seventh heaven and wanted to hug Pumpi. We however expressed our regrets to him though within our heart of hearts we were relieved and could not help feeling elated with victory at crossing the greatest hurdle.

2. Monster Vibhor

Monster *Vibhor* was born with an unusual capacity to work hard and he knew it. He was a bit egoistic (but all that did not matter in friendship). He was the topper of the class, son of a reputed businessman and so it was none of his fault if the stupid girls were drawn to him despite his fat figure (that's why we called him – Fatty) and a round face. He used to wear branded clothes (starting from his hair oil to the shoes were imported). Someone has rightly said that 'money speaks' and it did in his case. Sometimes I felt jealous of him at being so rich but at the end of the day, he was a great friend, who was always ready to give his blood for the sake of his friends. Moreover, the bank balance of his Dad provided financial backing and moral support to all our friends as his parents were always busy with their fucking social parties while he, determined not to take any help from his Dad, tried to live life according to his own rules; and he lived life to the fullest.

In libraries, it is a common sight to see sayings and quotations pasted on walls and racks and one of the most common is 'Books are our best friends', though we hardly think so about them. Vibhor was different. He believed that books were our best friends because they could extract us out of the most troublesome situations, including our exams, by providing all kinds of knowledge on all kind of things, but I could not understand why they could not help me in getting a girl...

Boys are great at maths (I agree I am not and maybe you too are like me, so it is nothing to worry about) and Vibhor was simply superb in maths. He could win any girl hands down with his extraordinary mathematical skill, which often made him enter into arguments with his teachers, who often could not counter his logic. He could make maths seem unimportant as most of the times he was busy creating new mathematical problems for himself and these were out of bounds for children like me. It had become common for us to hear the teacher tell him, "You'll understand it, but the class won't. So, better leave it rather than wasting the time of the class." But he could never get tired of it at all; instead, he seemed to thrive on solving new problems of the cosmos (he tried to expound on it to me, but I failed to understand it). He was considered Panini in maths and the princess was drawn towards him initially. She began to discuss problems very enthusiastically with him (problems which had always screwed me during the tests), who was smart enough to take advantage of the situation. During every free period, he was seen discussing some never-ending problems with her.

Moreover, he was an apogee of the corporate world with his more-than-necessary knowledge and Aprajita was the priestess of the temple, called the fake world. He used to explain to her the stories about how maths came to be discovered and she would willingly lap it all up. As was to be expected, she was trapped by him, or better still, by his mathematical knowledge. They both could be seen engrossed in the pages of *Business Today* and admiring some sadist faces wearing Armani suits. God alone knew what she saw in this! (I think she was the studious type) and was easily impressed by all the crap...

On the final day, as usual, they were busy discussing her mathematical problems in a free period, trying to solve an unsolvable problem, when the entire class chose to surround them to find out what was being discussed. "

"Look Aprajita, I don't want to do it but I have to. Sometimes you are pushed to take certain steps (I still wonder who could push the fatty so hard).

"What?" she asked with astonishment.

"I have begun to like you!" he said, bending down on his knees (it was a funny sight to see a fatty down on the ground in front of the princess and unluckily, I missed the incident as I was bound to the rules laid down by us monsters).

"No, Vibhor, it is not you. A career-oriented guy like you cannot fall for a girl in such a short period of time."

"Aprajita, it is me. Try to understand, there are some chapters, which shouldn't be revealed till the opportune moment," he begged.

"What? I don't get your point," she argued.

"No, you need not. It is all mixed up so much that even I cannot solve it easily. I myself am baffled at it, though I will never leave it midway. Please do give me your reply as I cannot leave without hearing your verdict."

"No, I cannot, but what is this crap that is doing the rounds that..."

"I'm bound to certain rules, otherwise I would have told you. I just want your answer. I really need it desperately."

"Vibhor, you know it by now. Are we not good companions?"

"Yeah we are."

"Then?" she replied evasively before lapsing into deep silence. Then she continued, "This week we discussed our career plans and I had thought that you were different. I know you are but I cannot continue with this relationship. I believe our relationship cannot continue for long as I do not see a future for it."

"Okay Aprajita, it is alright so long as we remain good friends. At least I have found someone who considers me intelligent and not a bookworm."

"No Vibhor, you are damn smart too."

"Sorry *yaar*. It was not at all intentional, but I cannot say anything more. Anyway, thank you for the compliment."

"No, there is no need for it, at least not now when we have entered into a bond of friendship," she said with a smile on her face (damn it, the lucky chap was present to witness a priceless smile).

We all kept waiting as our curiosity level had crossed the limit of patience, especially so because of his Dad's big bank balance (money is a magnet that can attract any magnet towards itself and scientifically it has been proved that the fairer sex gets drawn to it like a magnet. Oh God, I could not bear the tension any longer and wanted to scream).

We all were damn nervous as if we were about to enter the examination hall without any preparation for the final exams, so much so that we could not even recall our names.

Vibhor came towards us and divulged it all. He began, "Pumpi was right. She is studious and has the dream to master all kinds of skills."

"So, it was no, *nah*?" I asked as my patience was giving way to desperation.

"Yeah, obviously," he said in his casual, egoistic tone.

At this, Pumpi and Vibhor started discussing her like pompous guys who had got the chance to interact with the princess during the past two weeks. To boost my sagging morale, I told myself not to be unduly concerned because there was still the probability that I might succeed in wooing her. This did not mean that I was not worried about getting rejected because come to think of it, there was nothing special about me. But why was I thinking about her? After all, I did not love her or was it that I had been caught in the net woven by the four letters that were woven in love? I began to wait desperately for my turn to come. Oh God, please let her remain single for another week, so that I can get a chance to weave my magic on her.

3. Monster Shahid

Monster Shahid was a real champ. He was a savant, great mind with grit and determination to succeed in life. He played every game according to his own rules. He was largely unpredictable, went on cycle rides (without caring for the time) when he was either sad or happy. He was lauded by all the teachers as he had participated in the National Science Exhibition to present his project on the possibility of using herbal natural colours. He was a state-level basket-ball player (actually we both were defenders and had a good understanding among each other on the court. It was this quality which had strengthened our friendship, though I could only manage to get a place in the school team, he went on to become a state-level player) and the captain of the school cricket team. He was that unusual piece, who, if water flowed on his right, he would walk towards his left but still return with wet hands.

"If you do anything wrong and you are caught, that's called cheating but if you escape being caught and win the game, that's called experience, because it meants you can fool others and get what you want." That was Shahid for you.

Vibhor had already realised that he was not making much headway with the princess and thus was prepared for the outcome. But here was Shahid, who behaved as though he was not bothered about winning her attention but feared he might win on the final day. Initially we thought that Shahid had not made any success with her but smart as he was, he had got in touch with her on the very first day of school through his fake Yahoo ID under the name Arush and spent almost an hour with her. (I had a good mind to erase Yahoo for this cyber crime. How could this emotionless social website play such a cruel game with my lovely heart?) He has checked out on the girl from head to toe, discussing with her everything possible – movies, poems, childhood, inventions, career plans, social problems, etc. He had managed to impress the girl with the poems he had penned and I could not fathom why girls liked guys who could express their emotions on paper? We all knew that Shahid was a great poet and he even told her that he was from the same class as she was in but she could not place him.

On the final day, the day of the result (saturday of Monster Number-3), he reached an hour earlier in order to influence her in decision-making. I experieneed an unbearable pain to see them both giggle and whisper, share their thoughts, their nature and where they expected to reach after their three weeks' interaction. The one thing I realised that day was that my heart was burning with jealousy and my friends even told me, "You are able to accept a girl you like as the focus of attraction for each and every boy, but you are unable to accept the bombshell as your *bhabhi*." It was evident from the way they had been talking, chuckling at some inane topic, whispering into each other's ears and constantly smiling (it was all happening in front of my eyes and I did not know whether to be happy for my best friend or allow the long-awaited tears to flow down my eyes). I, however, was not willing to give up hope and told myself that there was still a chance for me. I guess I loved her, though I had observed that the two liked each other and had developed a strong bond. Now only a formal ceremony was required (to propose the girl on saturday), which according to tradition began on the basket-ball court, with the dude practicing with the ball in hand while fully concentrating on the girl (obviously you could not concentrate on a game with a sexy babe around and that is why Shahid and I never looked at the cheer girls when we entered the court to play and win). We had, however, been injured quite often for looking at babes who were in other schools because we were tired of seeing faces we got to see every day in our own school.

"What kind of boys do you have in your class?" she asked him.

"Are you talking about me?" he asked with his eyes wide open due to shock.

"No, you know about whom I am talking!" she said in an aggressive tone.

"Oh! Pumpi and Vibhor? They are trash. I had told you that they are jerks and do not discuss them. Just concentrate on the player in front of you and watch how he is practicing to show you his game."

"Stop flirting, Naanu!" she said, smiling (crap, he had told her his pet name, which I had thought I alone knew in the class).

All this while the player kept practicing all kinds of shots to impress her and these included lay up shot, jump, pointer, 3-D shot and all. I could only curse the bloody basket which had possibly vowed to swallow all the shots that he aimed into its mouth (I never knew the game could do such wonders as I had always played it for my passion). Aprajita kept staring at him with astonishment, standing next to the pole. Shahid tried to do the lay up running from half-court but missed it, caught the ball and jumped in front of her (only a few centimetres away from her), which made her move a few steps backward.

"Aprajita, I like you," he said, huffing loudly.

"You cannot!" she replied angrily (shit, they were just a few centimetres away).

"It is up to me to decide," he said in a supercilious manner.

"You must be joking! You had told me that you did not want to enter into any sort of relationship just a few moments ago."

"Yeah, you caught me on the wrong foot. I...."

"Tell me, why has all this crap been going on since the past three weeks – first Pumpi, then Vibhor and now you are doing the same? Is it a coincidence that is happening on every Saturday?"

"I cannot tell but you will get to know pretty soon," he said, taking his eyes away from hers.

"When? Tell me *nah*!"

"Maybe within a week!"

"If not, then Shahid, you will have to tell me."

"No, do not worry. You will definitely come to know it all."

The sword was now on my neck. I had done no preparations like Shahid and I knew that if I did try to get in touch with her, she would certainly get suspicious. Crap, it had all been messed up and I knew there was no way to escape. I wanted to propose to her but how was I to start?

The past—Girls will remain girls...

'Girls can only add twist and turns', someone has rightly said and that girls go totally crazy when they see something happening around them and want to get to know all the details, as if the universe would come to a stop if they did not get to know it. She discussed the entire scene with Gabby (one of my good friends), who was considered Mother India by the boys in the class and as Mother Teresa by the girls. She was straightforward, loved to go out with friends, broad-minded and could belt out all the possible abuses, like fuck, crap, jerk, asshole, etc. without flinching and it seemed she could not survive without using such words liberally.

Mother India obviously knew who were the brains behind it all and wanted to put my ass on fire with all the abuses at her disposal. She accompanied me to the school gate from the classroom and during this short walk belted out all the possible abuses that she could think of. She began, "Aditya, you bastard, have you already started your game on Aprajita?"

"No, I did not," I replied innocently as if she was my Mom and I her three-year old child.

"So you must be the next one to tackle her, you monster. You bloody rascals, just fuck off! Sometimes, I wonder how you could be my friend!"

"I'm sorry!" But all the apologies could not mean anything to her as she could not be won over that easily.

"Aditya, girls are not like you guys, totally mad and who indulge in activities without caring about the other's emotions. Have you ever thought of her? No and you can never become a boy from a monster. It is not a casual thing for a girl. If someone likes her, she gets to know of it for she can sense it. You guys have been doing this repeatedly with her since the past three weeks. You asshole, girls are sensitive about such matters and get disturbed. You guys have caught her in a maze and she is terribly worried at what is happening around her. You guys are really sick, you bloody monsters!"

"Listen to me, I can explain the situation to you," I stammered, while she kept on staring at me, her eyes blazing red hot flames.

"Shut up, you bastard," she screamed. People around us began to turn or stop to look at us. It became very embarrassing (especially when a sexy babe shouts at you in a crowd, it evidently means that you must have misbehaved with her to provoke her into screaming at you).

Obviously, after hearing the Rani of Jhansi spew fire at me, I stood with my head bent low as I did not have the guts to look into her fierce eyes, waiting to burn me down.

Finally, she left (thank God!) but after a warning, "I have told her about you monsters and your creepy game. It is a warning to keep away from her, else her brother is in our school in Class XII and he can make mincemeat of you all put together. So be careful about your next move. I am warning you as your friend."

I kept on wondering if it was a blessing or a death sentence! I felt depressed and humiliated and left the place, trying desperately to forget all that had transpired a few minutes earlier. But I could not escape from the reality.

Excerpts from My Diary

Someone has, rightly said. "Love is like a race in a circle, where you run behind yourself to search for the thing that you don't know whether it exists or not. You get carried away by everything before getting trapped."

It is time when I have started to realise that I love Aprajita. The situations have once again turned down the tables. I feel sorry for myself. I agree that my memorandum is not as great as my three lucky friends (they had the opportunity to interact with her before I could) but I want to give it a try at least. I loved her. This was the most pissing situation of my life when I was really desperate to propose to her but Mother India (the most dominating personality I have ever met) had screwed me. I could not betray her for she was a good friend.

Gabby was one of the girls, who had actually floored me (actually I must have been the most desperate guy on this earth to get clean-bowled by every other girl and that too physically). Like Aprajita, Gabby was the centre of the game called 'Get the Girl', when we were in Class VII. According to rules, I was the first monster to try it on her but she was not like any other girl. She slapped me on the first Saturday and that was the most embarrassing moment of my life. Her fingerprints are still fresh on my mind.

But as time passed, we grew up and became good friends because I happened to be an insensible guy and she was not a nun. She was the only girl with whom I would share all my feelings and she, being a girl, was obedient in responding the same way. She was straightforward in whatever she did (this is true and that was why she could make any boy dance to her tune). She was a very bold girl in school, the focus of all our talks and a sexy babe, but next to Aprajita. People thought she was a slut but I knew she was a great friend in every aspect, even in studies. Actually, she had kept my boat sailing in studies. What is more, the things that you can learn from life in the company of a girl cannot be learnt in any other way and the most important thing that I learnt from her was that 'every other girl on this earth is just another confused being' and she happened to be one of them.

She liked Pumpi and had told this to me thousands of times; she had however, failed to tell this to him, being an idiot that she was. So, I did not want to lose her as a friend. She was so important to me that I wanted to be with her all the time, be it in the canteen, during recess, on the basketball court, rocking in free periods in labs, killing boring time when you had to perform things that were beyond your immature mind and created by the greatest psychos born on this green planet. She was a good companion to spend time with and it was always great to have a sexy babe by your side. She was very sensitive too as she willingly helped the monsters to strengthen their friendship. She invariably helped us to go on adventure trips and I was sure that if she had not been a girl, she would have been a monster. We crazy boys adhered to rules. So according to our law, one had to be a boy to be a monster. I still remember she taught us how to abuse someone in a stylish manner.' "Just say 'adventure' in a strange tone with a tilted mouth and it would sound as an abuse but your hands would remain clean even after scratching another's ass."

I did not want to lose such a friend but Aprajita was one person from whom I could not take my eyes off. On seeing her, my heart started thumping at 200 beats per minute. Her cute face revolved in front of my eyes day and night; my thoughts were bound to her and my mind was busy thinking only about her. Whenever she was in front of my eyes, I just wanted to stare at her and whenever she was away, my thirsty eyes searched for her. I knew it was nothing but love. I loved her! Yes, I loved her. I knew she was the one for me. I had found the princess of my heart but the situations were not in my favour. I had to compromise with the heart and let the day end with the hope that everything would be alright when the sun shone next. I was really desperate to have her as my friend. Oh God, please show me the way...

Why couldn't I go in the past and change the order by becoming number one in the sequence of Monsters in the game, 'Get the Girls in a week'? At least then I could have talked to her, heard her beautiful voice, shook hands with her (I get excited at the mere thought of such things). I knew when three of the monsters known to me had tried to befriend her. Though none of them was serious about her, yet I was jealous. I did not know why? Why were my thoughts centred on her? Why was I worried at the thought of losing her, when I knew that she was not mine? I could not understand any of these things. However, fortunately for me, she was still single though I wondered how such a great girl could remain single! I wanted to talk to her but my blood frose when I thought of the bullets from AK-47 being fired at me by Mother India. Today I'm a maimed and helpless guy, who cannot follow his heart except to wait for the wound to heal and ask this cruel world to give me a chance to lead my life in my own way.

It would have been advisable for me to sleep because then I could see the princess in my dreams, where I was not a monster. I could keep gazing at her all the time. That would have been my life. She was the beginning of my race and also the end. But I was the defeated one and while she was the true winner. This Aprajita of mine.

Friendship drove me to divulge my desires to my friends with the result that I became the centre of amusement. It was all due to these bloody friends that I allowed myself to be caught in this web and now they made fun of me by calling me the 'trapped guy'. My heart proded me to lash out at them, if not thrash them, but then I told myself they were my friends. They seemed to me my arch rivals, these bloody bastard friends (who would stand and watch when you got involved in a fight; who sliced their pocket money to support you financially; who could even donate blood from their veins if you asked for it. Ironically the same friends could forget all this if the topic was girls. We all decided to move on with our great tasks and ignore the new bombshell.

It may have been easy for them to take off their eyes from her but how could I? I could not curb myself from staring at her. Ignoring her was next to impossible for me though friendship teaches you everything. It had taught me to care for others and to live for a relation who had nothing to do with blood. It taught me to live in every kind of situation, be it of sorrow or laughter. But I hate to admit it that all such philosophies have proved futile. I just loved her. She was ravishingly beautiful and I was a monster. I had to tolerate the other monsters, whether I liked it or not.

The next day we discovered that Aprajita had gone, she was no more a buzz. We all were devastated. They could exist without seeing her, but I just could not. Her daily routine was to come and sit on the very first bench by the window. Undoubtedly she was the most impressive student in the class. She excelled in her studies, a strong rival to Vibhor with whom she was often seen talking (girls are never excellent at maths, which was the subject of their discussion. Thank God, Aryabhatta is not alive or these girls would have used him thousands of times). Shahid had exchanged some formal notes with her and which she had answered just for the heck of it. Pumpi had found another girl in the other section. That left me as the only one who had not even heard her voice properly, or seen her fetching smile, or shook hands with her. Leave alone that,

I must have been the only guy who had never even faced her directly since her first day in class. I have thought, Oh Lord, are you judging my friendship or conveying to me that I am not destined to be with her?

What could I tell my innocent heart to make it happen? If we are not destined to be together, I cannot fight Destiny. I however wanted to give it a try, in the hope of making her destiny be mine. I could dream of a life with her. I daydreamt about the day when I would get to know her, hear her heart-throbbing voice, look into her seductive eyes and hear my name being called by her. I was lost in this ethereal world, a different world. Would it ever happen? Was I becoming mad in love?

The one thing that I was certain about was that my monster friends had really destroyed my love-life. But then, they were my friends and friendship has to withstand everything….

The usual routine continued for the next six months till the 'festival of lights' or Diwali came. These monster friends were planning on launching a bomb attack in Class IX. We were not terrorists, although we had heard that efficient terrorists had once been good students. It was just that with time, you acquire experience and there always were moneyed hands behind to offer assistance if you got caught. However, being in Class IX, we were happy to be 'human bombs' only.

Awesome! We are, awesome, we do...

This evidently meant that we were quite different from the rest of the world and our actions were a xerox copy of our name. It was a simple plan to throw a bomb in the class but when it had to be executed by monsters, it had to be done in a special way. Actually it had to be done technically and in the most economical way. This meant that create the maximum havoc with the minimum of effort. We had to execute the task in front of Hitler (teacher) himself.

Like any other plan, we had to follow certain rules to execute the plan so that it would make every human tremble with terror and freeze the blood of Paploo (that's what we called our principal). The instructions for our master plan were:

- A human bomb had to be placed inside the dustbin and a hole pierced in it by using a pair of scissors and fire. The free end of the thread and the starting edge of the bomb was be passed on to the first bench.
- The plan was to be executed during the very first period. The preparations could easily be done before school hours. Moreover, after the first period, the dustbin would be full with wrappers and other trash material, which could extinguish the fire.
- The person to impart life to our dreams had to sit on the very first bench which was considered the least vulnerable and with the least chance of raising any doubt in the teacher. The one who would ignite the fire had to be the one to make the game begin. The hero executing the job from the first bench was to be given the same lighter with which to launch the bomb attack in the small 36 x 12 ft hamlet.

On the final day, the monsters, feeling tense and nervous, had to perform the most difficult task of proving who they were and what were their capabilities. We reached the class an hour before time with all the required material. Shahid started drilling a hole in the dustbin and was over with it in the next ten minutes. Then he placed the bomb at the designated spot with the thread running to the first bench where I was expected to sit. I was the most trusted monster for execution of any plan because they believed that I was blessed with a great sense of humour which was very important if you were to get caught. However, I knew that they only needed a culprit to carry out their plan. In any case I enjoyed carrying out such tasks because they required *ulta dimaag* (brain), the *dimaag* with which I was blessed. We filled the dustbin with some trash, keeping the level not more than that of the bomb. We stood all around the dustbin to prevent anyone from coming near it. A lighter was handed over to me by Shahid who wished me with the words, "Today, our pride, respect, honour and dignity lies in your hands, so just go ahead and prove to them all that you are a monster."

It was necessary to divulge our plan to the one seated next to me and that happened to be Gabby. I still do not know why are plan went awry. Sometimes a plan can take a turn for the worst and at times it can turn out to be great.

What happened next? You may call it a providential accident or a counter plan by someone, who actually knew my condition. Aprajita entered and kept her bag down on the same first bench (how lucky that bag was to cover her body, slide down on her skin and be touched by her hands. If she had been ready to accept me as her bag, I would have been too delighted to oblige.) As she had been seated next to me, I had to reveal our plan to her.

"Hi Aprajita!" I said excitedly (actually I couldn't control the joy of talking to her for the first time in my life).

"Hi!" she replied in a sassy way.

"That seat is reserved for me," I said, trying to regain my beaten senses by this unbeaten girl.

"How come a rock-star has started solving mathematical problems"? she asked in a taunting voice. No matter whatever crap she puked out, I was floored. If she had told me to kick my own ass, I would have attempted it. I was completely out of my brains with regard to her. But all she did was to fire some bullets of AK-47 at me. I managed to control my senses and gather my guts to blabber, "We have got a plan."

"What sort of a plan?" she asked.

"As Diwali is just three days away and it would be our last day in school before the festival....."

I was trying to build the confidence to speak to her, but she interrupted, "You are planning to plant a bomb in the class?"

"Are you a witch?" I stammered, astonished at her sudden reaction.

"No *yaar*! It is the most probable plan you monsters can think of. Even a dim-wit can guess about it and everyone has been awarded an *ulta* (perverted) brain," she yelled.

"Can I..." I stammered again. It was likely to happen when you were being continuously gazed at by a mind-blowing beauty, who could rob you of all your thoughts in one go. I loved her anyway.

"Wait! Wait a minute! What's your plan?" she asked curiously. She looked so cute when peering at me like a three-year old child and I realised she looked most beautiful when her eyes showed curiosity.

"You will come to know gradually, madam. Just allow me to sit next to you and enjoy the game," I replied forcefully.

We both sat on the first bench and I explained the plan to her. Meanwhile the first period started and all the monsters moved to their different seats. Aprajita and I sat together on the bench to rock the class, that is, to shake the brains of every idiot in the class with the thread placed under my shoe. One by one, each of my bastard friends began to signal to me to light the fire, but I could not take off my eyes from the extreme beauty seated at my side. Her long black hair rolled down to her waist, her pink lips, her sexy legs and the black spot below her lips simply flunked me. She seemed more and more beautiful with each passing day or may be God had blessed her with the magical power to capture the senses of every boy. I was fascinated by her beauty. Here she was seated next to me, staring at the bloody teacher as I stole glances at her every now and then, looking completely mesmerised at her ravishing beauty.

She placed her foot on mine, reminding me of my mission. Who was interested in the mission when she was seated next to me? All I wanted to do was to look at her. It was on moments like these that being a monster was not at all easy. I took out the lighter from my pocket and moved my hand towards the thread. Crap, my hands were trembling (for the first time in my life) for no reason, while my fellow monsters were signalling to me to light the fire. I was completely blind to the atmosphere around me. I had taken leave of my senses. This had happened for the first time in my life. I don't know! How she realized my condition and suddenly, she snatched the lighter from my hand and performed the job. She was so brave and smart. I wondered how she could still be unattached and single! She left the lighter below our bench and I quickly bent down to retrieve it. The count-down had already started (with the fire travelling from the first bench to the dustbin) – 10, 9, 8, 7, 6, 5, 4, 3, 2, 1 and a loud blast – a heart-wrenching noise that resounded in the corridor, replacing the complete silence. The teachers in the classes around ceased scratching their chalks on the blackboards and stood dumbstruck, as if turned to statues. All the monsters enjoyed it all and squealed with shouts of joy and breaking the agony of the silence.

The dustbin was shattered to pieces and the rooms filled with smoke. The students jumped out of their seats as if their seats had been set afire at the same time. Chaos and complete mess prevailed with students running helter-skelter, shouting and whistling. It was at that very moment that I dropped the lighter in the purse of our teacher.

If you enter a temple with shoes on or with a weapon to attack, it can be dangerous enough to shake even the largest democracy in the world. This proved so true when the Operation BlueStar cost the late Prime Minister Indira Gandhi her seat. So we were just the 16-year old terrorists who had bombed the temple of knowledge. Strict action was going to be taken against us as a result. In the next two minutes all the students were told to empty their classes by the senior teachers. Paploo, our principal and our class teacher stood in front of us, asking us, "Who the hell is responsible for all this?" Evidently they were trying to scare us by threatening to meet out the most serious punishment to the mastermind of this attack but it is in moments like these that unity rocks! We all stood silently, oblivious to their threats. We monsters were proud of what we had done. It was our greatest achievement to light a bomb in the class in the presence of a teacher. The hapless teachers, left with no other option, began to search our pockets, bags and desks, and whatever they could think of checking. I looked at Aprajita and noticed the worried look on her face. She had suddenly remembered that she had left the lighter below our desk. She looked so worried that tears filled her eyes, waiting to flow out any moment and she looked so beautiful that I could not take my eyes off her face. In a very low tone she whispered, "I am worried for you Aditya. They will catch you but not me as they trust me fully." If we had not been in the class, I would have definitely kissed her. Not only did she look cute but she also cared for me. She continued to look wistfully at me, "What is going to happen?"

I nodded at her sadly as if I knew that I had been awarded the punishment to be hanged till death.

Aprajita kept silent during the entire operation, sweating profusely while our desks were being checked. I could hear her pray to God, blinking her eyes and trying to avoid looking at all that was happening around her.

Despite a very minute search, nothing incriminating could be found except for a pair of scissors in Shahid's bag and which he claimed he had brought for some work in the lab on a project.

They all left the class after announcing a mass punishment to all of us. We all were made to stand outside Paploo's office for one complete day and were insulted in front of the entire school, after the assembly. We monsters loved such a punishment because it allowed us to stand on the stage in front of all the sexy girls, who looked admiringly at our courageous acts. We indeed had become the show-stealers and personally I was happy because the monsters had always been looked down upon as the masterminds behind such incidents. Aprajita kept staring at me suspiciously for the next few seconds and then yelled, "What? How?"

I simply winked at her and replied confidently, "They will find it soon."

Soon everyone came to know that the lighter had been found in our teacher's bag. Later on, when Aprajita came to know about the whole episode and the brain behind it all, she was visibly impressed at my courage to place it inside teacher's bag and she expressed her appreciation at my sense of humour. Either it was my *ulta dimaag* which had to be appreciated or her *ulta* brain.

Was the game over...

If anyone had asked me at that point of time as to what could have been the most difficult job in the world, undoubtedly my answer would have been, "To get the girl."

The game which was supposed to get over within four weeks was still continuing and I was still waiting for the Saturday to come, when I could tell Aprajita how I felt when I saw her; how I struggled each day to escape the heart attack when she smiled at me; how cute she looked when she laughs as if bells rang in a temple and how endearing the dimples in her cheeks looked, carrying me away to another world in which only we both live. It was a world in which no one else lived except for us who had no identity but had the freedom to do nothing else but to gaze into each other's eyes, wordlessly and endlessly; a world where emotions had taken a lead over the spoken word; a world no matter where I looked, I saw her everywhere. In each and every breath of mine there existed an unspeakable name and I could not tell how that world had become my life. I did not know whether such a world existed or not but I could imagine living in such a world with her, gazing into her eyes and discovering her likes and dislikes. I wanted to get lost in her.

I discovered that I wanted to stare at her and store the memory of her beauty in my mind because such beauty was forever a source of sublime pleasure. Her every small act, her dimpled smile, her way of talking, her shy glance at me were enough to send my senses reeling. I loved to bask in this adventurous journey from exchange of side glances to building a deep bond of friendship. Someone has very aptly put, "If you do the job you love to do, you will not have to work a single day in your life." Yes, it was nothing but the truth. I enjoyed planning about the chance I would get to talk to Aprajita the next day. I planned to reach the school an hour before time and sit next to her, doing every task assigned in class. My love for her had been increasing day by day.

The game was not over yet because I had not had the opportunity to propose to her. I desperately waited for the Saturday to come when I hoped to propose to her. At times I wondered if I could muster the courage to pop the question to her ever!

Would this game ever end or would I just keep roaming like a street dog? I had a number of questions to put to her as I had no answer to them. I had many options in my mind but did not know which would be the right one. Like an idiot, I kept on thinking of the question that was uppermost in my mind and hoped fervently that I would get an answer one day when the game could end…

Yahoo! Yippee!...

February, 2004

'Bye! 'Bye Class IXth!

Like any other school, our school authorities thought that students could do great wonders if given more time in Class X, but I wanted to remind them, more meant more. It took Albert Einstein his whole life to perform great wonders in science; Bill Gates left his education midway to become the richest man on earth; Dhirubhai Ambani screwed his school life to follow his dreams; but we were here in this cruel world, which believed in shortcuts; where the teachers expected very student to earn name and fame by scoring good marks in the Boards (at the expense of causing us Board phobia). I was aware that the teachers would never accept this in front of the society as they had nurtured us from seeds to make us grow into helpful trees, although in my case the reverse had transpired as I have ended in becoming a monster. How could I forget that I was a grown-up boy who would not like to screw up his Class IX result or be unconcerned about not faring well? We all tried to give it the best shot that we could. I just want to ask the stupid people a simple question, "Isn't the greatest shot played by a normal ball, without any extra preparation?" So why the hell should they do this to us? We have got to move with the music and here I was turning my ass hot, scratching it against my bed as the session was to start the following week.

The phone rang...

"Hi Buddy, what's up?" Shahid asked in an energetic tone, reminding me of the school days when we made fun of each other with the same vibrant energy.

"Nothing. Just thinking of what could be as sexy as I could ever think."

"So, Aprajita must be at the top!"

I remained silent for the next two seconds, as he was right, but how the hell did he know about it? After all, he was just my friend, but then, a friend can give you much more than you could ever expect.

"No, actually it's a BMW," I said, continuing the conversation in order to get back to my normal state of mind.

"I never knew you were thinking of marrying a car. You are really different from the rest of this world. But Mr Alien, can we keep your extraordinary character aside to discuss something more important?"

"Yeah, the bloody, helpless earthly guy, we can." (I felt like Jadoo in the Hindi movie '*Koi mil Gaya*', the guy from the other planet, with extraordinary powers.) Unfortunately, bound as I was to the gravitational force of the earth, science could always drag me to reality, no matter how much I exercised my imagination to go away from the planet Earth.

"It's Fatty's birthday tomorrow and he is very disturbed right now due to an argument with his parents. As his friends, we need to do something about it."

"How can I help you, Shahid?"

"Look, Fatty has gone out to play snooker and I am planning to take a cake to his house..."

I interrupted, "But what's so special about it?"

"Just shut up! I will keep the cake hidden in some corner of his house and ask him to find the gift at 00:00 hours."

"So, what do you want me to do?"

"I want Fatty to hear about this gift from the lips of a girl and I have been trying Gabby's number since the past one hour but she is not picking the call up. Shall I try the second best option and which is Aprajita?"

"You want me to call her?"

"No, no! I want you to recite her name all night long, dumbo. Obviously. I would have done the job myself but neither am I a close friend of hers as to persuade her to stay awake till 12 at night, nor is Fatty so smart as to prod her to do the job. So the only victim left is you because she is with you most of the time and I can give you her number." He disconnected after giving me her number.

As soon as he had disconnected, I began to wonder if I was a victim or a conqueror and if the world would like to call me a victim and be ready to be hanged till death for the crime of giving away my innocent heart to a princess! I had her number on a piece of paper in my hand – the ten digits which could take me to my world – the world where I always wanted to get lost. These digits could help me listen to the magical voice – the voice which had the ability to drive me crazy and make me jump to infinity. That was the magic of my love. I kept looking at her number for the next ten minutes for no rhyme or reason. I just enjoyed getting lost in those ten digits, my hands clasped tightly around that bit of paper. Thank you, science, for having helped to create the communication network that could connect us to each other. Just a few moments earlier how I hated science but now, I had come to love it because it could take me to my love. Either I had become mad or my love had made me crazy.

Finally, on returning back to the earth, I realised that I needed to call the princess. Already afloat in the seventh sky, I did call her. The bell kept on ringing and ringing, giving me the time to think of what I would say to her when she picked up the phone. My mind was busy debating if she would agree to what I would tell her! Though all kinds of thoughts crowded in my mind, confusing it more than it already was, I could not help but enjoy it all.

She was not picking the call. I hoped she would pick it up if I rang up again. So I tried the same number again and again at least five times but all in vain. No reply!

Somewhat perplexed and not knowing what to do despite having the phone in my hand with the ten magical digits in it, there was no way I could start my conversation with her. Hoping against all hope of talking to her, I began to plan how I would begin the dialogue and what all I would ask. Normally in such situations, when nothing else worked, it was my *ulta dimaag* which came to my aid. Yes a brainwave travelled through my mind and I decided to message her the following message: 'Hi Aprajita! This is Aditya, I gt ur no. 4m Shahid. I nd 2 tk most urgent.'

Before ten seconds could pass, my cell phone flashed, 'You have a text message' and as expected, it was from her.

'Me vd prnts. Cnttk ryt nw, vl cl u.' I could not help but wonder how quickly the girls could type a message! It took me more than two minutes to type the message but she was ready with a reply within ten seconds. After all she was my princess!

I waited for her call, wondering how her voice would sound on the phone! Could it be as seductive as she was or would she sound even better than that? After all the world rests on hope and I being a lover boy, could only wait and hope to hear her voice on the phone.

At 22:30, my phone rang and I jumped, expecting to hear her voice. But as bad luck would have it, it was Shahid on the line.

"Have you talked to Aprajita?" he asked in an aggressive tone.

"No, she's not picking up, but I have messaged her and she has promised to call back. So I am waiting for her call," I told him.

"Okay tell her to call from an unknown number because Fatty already has her number. Also, ask her to sound a bit different, that is, more seductive in order to excite him. Do tell her not to reveal her identity as I am planning a surprise party for him tomorrow."

"She's not my servant! How can I ask her that? And what's so special?" I asked in the same voice.

"You have to and there is a big plan for tomorrow."

"What is it?" I squeaked excitedly.

"Nothing much; may be a movie or something like that."

"Are you going to invite Aprajita?" I asked with a wildly beating heart. I had no control over my emotions. I really wanted to know beforehand so that I could dress up accordingly.

"Yeah, as she will be carrying out the tough job. All the monsters, apart from Gabby and Aprajita, will reach Fatty's place by 10 in the morning."

"What? We'll keep Fatty in suspense till the next morning?"

"Yes, let the bastard enjoy the special day."

"Shahid, you're such a...."

"Hey, that's what I am," said Shahid and put down the phone.

It is at moments like these that you realise the importance of friends. It is they who are willing to do anything impossible to make you feel important. I vividly remember one of my birthdays when my friends dialled every other friend to remind them that it was my birthday and that I was not in a happy mood. They transformed one of my unhappiest days into a most happening one. That's why Shahid was one of the best friends (available 24 x 7 and at any hour) and he wanted to keep Fatty in suspense.

A call came from Aprajita. “Hi, Aditya!” she said. The two words sounded like music to my ears. They were so seductive that they could bring the zenith to my feet. I remained silent for a few seconds because I could not believe that I was hearing her voice. It reminded me of the days when I used to dream of her and doze off on my bed, with the magical ten digits reassuring me that it was her.

“Hi..A...Aprajita!” I stuttered.

“So, what’s the important thing?” she asked.

“Hey! Do you know it’s Fatty’s birthday tomorrow?”

“Yup, I know!”

“How can you? Are you a witch?” I did not know what made me say that but then I told myself, after all she was in my class, so there was nothing wrong in calling her that.

“I do have my sources, Aditya.”

“Yeah, actually we have a plan for the party. Shahid has kept the cake at Fatty’s place and you need to call him from an unknown number and order him to search and find the gift in his own house.”

“What are you monsters trying to do?” she asked. It really sucks when your group name dominates your personal identity.

“We want it to be a special treat for him and you must keep your identity a secret. Fatty is liable to get excited and we have seen that girls are the ultimate solution to any problem. Remember not to call from your number as Fatty has your number.”

“Okay, give me his number.”

The plan rocked and it had to because it had been chalked out by Shahid. So, as per our plan, we all, except for Aprajita, wished him at 12 o'clock at night. Aprajita rang him up from an unknown number, asking him to find the gift that had been hidden in his house. Fatty began to search like a lost guy in his own house. She added a twist to the plan by asking him to search in the drawer of the study table, below the bed, in the almirah, in his school bag or in the washroom. He really searched for it like a mad guy, with even his parents helping him search for it. They too seemed to be enjoying the excitement. Finally the game got over when his birthday began at 1:30 in the morning and he located the gift in the letter-box hung on the gate. He was thrilled to see the beautifully packed cake and immediately rang up the unknown number from which Aprajita had rung up to thank for the gift. By this time he had guessed who were the culprits – it had to be the monsters because who else would have thought of doing such a thing?

I was about to doze off on my bed, when my phone flashed 'A new text message.'

'Thnx 4 mkin it so spcl. He njoyd it ol. It's grt fun, you monsters really rock. Monsters actually mean a nw name to d friendship. I njyd it ol. Thnx.'

I replied, 'We r grt 4 2 thngs – girls n frndship.'

She wrote back, 'Dat's y u askd me 2 do d job.'

I sent her, 'Fatty is jst nothr monster, mad 4 gals.'

She wrote back, 'All d monsters r mad 4 gals.'

I sent her, 'That's wt defines us.'

She sent, 'Don't u lyk ny grl in prticulr?'

The flirtation was at its peak and I always enjoyed such moments, though this time it was something special. I was feeling the love in everything around me, even in the phone.

I felt the love waves getting conveyed from my phone to hers, taking the message of my heart to her heart to convey my feelings, directly from my pumping machine to incite some movement in hers...

I sent to her, 'Ya!Thr's 1, d unbeaten.'

She shot back, 'Who's d lucky 1?'

I wrote, 'Nt jst lucky; d luckiest. Her name starts with the letter A and ends with the same.'

She wrote back, 'She's really lucky!'

I sent her, 'Ny1 in ur lyf?'

She sent, 'No m stl waiting 4 d 1 2 drive me crazy.'

I sent her, 'All the best! n kp ur eyes open.'

She wrote, 'K gud 9t!'

I sent her, 'Thnx n think 4 d lucky 1.'

Our messaging came to an end and I realised that if I ever entered into a relationship with her, it was going to be damn difficult as she, with her speed of typing messages would send me two while I would still be on the first one as I would just be thinking of what to write. She seemed to be participating in a race to fill up the inbox section of the opposite player.

Crap, either I needed to tighten my belt or had to prepare myself to lose the battle every time. But once she was with me, I was ready to take up any challenge or to be beaten by the unbeaten, that is, Aprajita. The other thing that kept troubling my mind were the names starting with A and ending with A, like Anamika, Anika, Akansha, Aastha, Arpita, Ananya, Anisha, Aashima and others. I wondered why I could think of so many names but never the name Aprajita! Why was it that she could not gauge what my heart felt, especially when she had the name beginning with an A and ending with an A?

Next day, we all went to a movie and lunch offered by Vibhor. It gave us the opportunity to bathe in the sea of love, especially me as I could happily observe each and every cute action of hers that helped to intensify my love for her.

I was deeply in love……

Finally it was my turn...

Since that day we became good friends and found that we had the same habits, loved watching same movies, discussing our individual philosophies, forgetting the world when undertaking any task, living life in our inimitable manner, net surfing and all. Most of our time passed in discussing what we really wanted to do and this included conquering the Himalayas in our dreams and breaking each and every shackle imposed by the society.

One thing that I learnt on getting to know her was that girls do not get impressed if you have similar likes and dislikes but like it if both hate the same things. That is how our friendship grew stronger and stronger, making fun out of each and every moment, establishing an unbreakable bond. We enjoyed making fun of things we did not like. We both stayed together in school, trying to discover the lost ends of our minds. We talked about our families, likes, dislikes, movies, fashion, people, childhood – everything possible that we could think of. We needed just about anything to discuss all day and night. Thanks to the facility of 'Yahoo', as our phone bills reached an all-time high. We enjoyed talking for no apparent reason; we did never get enough of it and we both kept growing emotionally. We became addicted to exchanging messages or talking on the phone – I to get the chance to listen to her endearing voice and she for reasons unknown to me. I came to such a pass that I began talking to her even in my sleep.

I found that our relationship got strengthened because we began to make the other feel important by giving more time, lending ear to hear the other's problems and developing an extraordinary emotional bond that could actually connect us even telepathically. It has been seen that the moment you become addicted to a person's voice, you begin to feel their breath in your own body. You can actually judge their condition just by looking at them and get worried for them. You begin to smile without any reason by just remembering them. You long to catch a glimpse of the other person without bothering about who is around or who is watching you, whether it's day or night, whether you are awake or asleep. The face of your love keeps appearing in your mind every day and night. Here let it be remembered that is what I felt and I hoped she felt the same about me too. We had indeed become good friends.

Theory exams are not always to write and accomplish...

August 7, 2004

One year passed and our friendship grew with every passing day. We had become good friends.

When studying, it was seen that some subjects captured all our attention and we enjoyed reading them from the bottom of our heart but there were some subjects which, no matter how much we studied, we could not enjoy them. One such subject was EVS (Environmental Science), which was an optional subject but was included in the syllabus possibly to keep us away from all kinds of pleasure. It must have been included merely to add another paper in the examination date-sheet and give employment to a greater number of teachers as the school had plenty of funds to spare.

Shahid and I were sitting in my home, spending another sleepless night, preparing for the fucking exams. I just could not bring myself to concentrate on my studies because my mind was preoccupied with thoughts of Aprajita. As Shahid was my best friend, I used to share my thoughts and feelings about her with him, thus preventing him also from studying for his papers.

"I like her!" I began.

"What's the response from the other side?" he asked like a saint.

"I don't know, *yaar*"! I replied sedately.

"Any idea?"

"No *yaar*!"

"It's great news! My best friend has finally got floored by a girl," he said laughingly (though 'excitedly' would be a better word to describe his response).

"Cool down, buddy. I don't know whether it is love or infatuation. You know me, *nah*! I am a bastard; I don't believe in a relationship. I consider them merely restrictions imposed on us and worth a dime. We are simply good friends. She is smart and beautiful and any guy can be floored by her. She is a topper in class and is not studious but intelligent. She is a career-oriented girl. I find her equally cute when she behaves like a three-year child or as a mature adult. She has actually changed the image of girls in my eyes and I no longer consider them silly. Quite possibly she is an exception. And I am an idler; my face is covered with pimples; I am just muck in comparison to her. I have become an insomniac; I spend all my time reminiscing about the time spent with her and still feel that she is the one but not merely for me." I felt quite relieved on opening out to Shahid with all this information.

"You are in love with her," he said.

"Every boy on this earth can fall in love with her after knowing her. I am merely one of them," I said in a serious voice.

"Crap, she loves you too," he affirmed with conviction (an over-aggressive Shahid said.)

"How can you say that?"

"Just think. Does she behave in the same manner with the others?"

I remained silent because he undoubtedly was correct. "Just now you said that anyone can fall in love with her after knowing her. In that case, does she allow anyone else to be a part of her life as you are? Has she revealed her strengths and weaknesses to anybody else? You're the special one, dumbo, with whom she discusses it all. You both are lost in your own world when you are together. Have you ever seen her behaving in the same manner with any other guy? She likes you but it is possible that she has not realised it so far," he said.

I could not believe my ears that all this was being said by one of my bastard friends who seemed pretty dense to me.

"But we are just good friends," I squeaked.

"Okay, do you want to check it out? Just pick your phone and dial her number," he said aggressively.

"But, what do you want me to do?" I asked politely.

"Just do what I say," he commanded. How could I oppose Shahid, especially when I was behaving like a fool in front of him?

The phone kept on ringing with my heartbeats increasing in crescendo. Scientifically I did not know what was happening around me. (I guess where love starts, science ends.)

"Hello!" she said. Her sweet voice was no less intoxicating than any wine.

"Hi Aprajita! What's up? Missing me *nah*? I know you and if you're not, then put the phone down, you shameless friend." (What had come upon me that I was speaking like this to her?)

"Yeah, I was dying to hear your voice. If you are free to talk to me, the pleasure is all mine." (I could never win against her in the play of words.)

"Actually, I was quite busy looking after the new models of BMW..."

She interrupted, "Hey, what does BMW stands for? I have always heard BMW only and have never known the full form."

Fortunately, I knew it, so I bragged, *"Bayerische Motoren Werke."*

"Is that English?"

"Wait a minute!" I turned to Shahid to ask what to say to that. He was busy writing something on a piece of paper but he turned to me to say, "Just read this out as it is, keeping your brain aside."

I told her, "Can you give me Gabby's new number?"

"No, I don't have it but why do you need it now?" she asked.

"When I looked at my life, I discovered that I have not proposed to any girl so far. So, I am going to propose to her," I stammered and threw daggers at Shahid, who signalled to me to continue. Like a faithful dog, I continued, "I am going to propose to all the girls, who have been my crush."

"What?" she squeaked. (I guess the plan was working.)

"How many are there?" she screamed.

"Just five or six," I replied nonchalantly.

"What, if any one of them was to say 'yes'?"

"No, no one will as I trust myself and my absurd nature. No girl can say 'yes' to me."

"You are wrong Aditya. As a girl, if I was asked the same question, I would have said, 'yes'."

I was overwhelmed and found myself floating on cloud nine. The earth slipped under my feet and I lost myself completely in what was happening around me.

Shahid broke into my world by shouting out to me, "Aditya?"

"Hey! Who is that?" she asked.

"It is Shahid. He is at my place to study with me."

"So, you are going to study?"

"Yeah I have to. Even the books are really desperate to get the pleasure of seeing us two handsome dudes go through their pages. We are just obliging them."

"So, give as much pleasure to the books as you can but do ensure that both the books and you are completely satisfied," she said, bursting into laughter.

"I'll take care of that. Now I must sign off as someone is quite desperate to be with me. 'Bye and best of luck for tomorrow's exam."

As I put the phone down and turned to Shahid, who had been glaring at me so far, he burst out like a dormant volcano, "Got the proof?"

"I don't know. Maybe she is trying to please me by saying that I am not bad as a boyfriend," I said as I was unsure of her.

"You are so dumb and useless. Even God cannot make you realise that you are in love and she likes you."

He began to study his EVS book silently but angrily, as I got busy trying to study the relationship between her and me and finding it unfavourable to myself. I began to think that my *ulta dimaag* would have to help me get me through my exams. I began to recollect all those happy moments I had spent with her and how we had drawn close to each other, cementing our relationship in an unbreakable bond. But as I was conscious of my limitations, I was not sure if she really cared for me and decided to go all out and solve the mystery of whether it was love or just friendship.

The exams begin...

The exams began and I decided to tick all the questions to get through the exam. I would have been happy to score even a C-grade. I looked carefully at the question paper and discovered I was done for. My blood froze, body turned numb, brain got lost and my *ulta dimaag* refused to provide me some clue when I needed it most. The paper was full of definitions, though the other students told me that all the topics had been given in the syllabus. But how could I know this as I had not even bothered to see the syllabus? I asked one fellow seated next to me, “Can anyone tell me what is the colour of my EVS book?”

The definition was to be followed with a brief explanation and the paper consisted of only five words (eutrophication, ten per cent law, etc. but I had not even seen the face of the EVS teacher as I had bunked all the classes). Those five fucking words held my neck in their hands.

I felt it would be unbearably embarrassing to fail in EVS, so I looked around and found every lucky guy busy writing, letting their knowledge-bird fly. I felt tied to my bench. I looked at my teacher and felt she was not more than 30-years old but she had a strong grudge against me. (I had coined the name *Dian* out of her original name 'Diana' due to her characteristics). Unfortunately, she knew this all and was not going to let go of this chance to screw me.

I was willing to call her Mother Teresa, provided she allowed me to cheat in the exam. She was continuously staring at me and I had no other option except to look at my princess, Aprajita, who was wholly responsible for my situation as it was she who kept on occupying my heart and brain, never allowing me to concentrate on my studies. I thought I was on my way to creating history in the school's record as 'the only student to excel in failing in the EVS exam – Aditya Relhan.' It was to be a great honour.

Aprajita was busy writing reams of papers in the exam while I kept gazing at her, happy to see her know her subject. I was not like that teacher to hold grudges and not mature enough to forget the past and move on. I just wanted to discover Aprajita's limitless beauty. That teacher would never find anything good in me because as someone has said, 'Beauty lies in the eyes of the beholder', and it was not her fault that she could not discover any good in me.

Wake up boy! Suddenly a brainwave travelled through my damn creative mind and I got it! Yippee! I got it. I wrote down on the answer sheet, "After studying this subject very deeply right from the bottom of my heart, I have come to realise that I would be the greatest fool on my green planet to waste such an important resource of Nature just to earn a few useless marks. The time to act is NOW; remember THERE'S NO PLANET-B."

At the end of the paper, tears began to roll down my cheeks and Aprajita noticed them. She came to me and said in a sympathetic tone, "Baby, whatever you've written, you will get marks for it and I know you will top in the exam because of your unusual sense of humour." (Undoubtedly, she was a witch. She must have been aware that I had screwed my paper and was now trying to console me.) I wanted to slap her because I felt she was making fun of me but she was a princess – Aprajita Khanna.

I reached home in a depressed mood and immediately dropped on my bed, reminiscing about the good old times when I used to top in class. I was actually trying to overcome the shock that I would fail in EVS (the easiest subject). I realised that the fear of failure is very difficult to face. But the trouble is that this world does not allow you to cry even.

Aprajita rang up and chirped, "So, you have topped in EVS, dude."

"Oh, shut up! Are you nuts or something? How can I get any marks?"

"Is everything alright?" she asked in her usual cute voice.

"No! I have screwed my exams. Anyway, who the hell told you this?" I asked, though not believing her words.

"The teacher has told me. I visited her in the last period and she told me that I could not top this time because a boy named Aditya had done an excellent job. She was really curious to see you because according to the attendance records, you had not attended a single class of hers."

"I am sure you are joking. It is impossible. I had written just two lines in my whole paper," I said. I was not merely surprised to hear all that she told me, I was simply shocked and overwhelmed.

"Yep! Those two lines were more than enough to floor the teacher, who appreciated your answer and was surprised that you knew nothing on the subject. She was impressed by your attitude and told me that when she had appeared for her IAS exam, she had been given to write an essay on laziness and she had filled ten sheets, pouring out all her knowledge on the sheet. She was rejected but the guy who actually made it to IAS, left all the sheets blank and wrote one single line, saying, 'This is called laziness.' According to her, you have got the same attitude. I asked her to show your answer sheet but she said that your attitude needed to serve as an example to all the other students in the class, so we will have to wait till Monday."

"I still can't believe that my attitude has really turned the tables in my favour," I said very proudly.

"It's your attitude that has really drawn me to you, you idiot."

"So, now I can have a good weekend and will go out for tennis as there's nothing special to do."

"*Besharam*, tomorrow is my birthday," she said angrily and put the phone down without hearing a single word. Actually the fault was mine as I was so engrossed in my own world that I had forgotten about her.

Oh crap, how could I forget her birthday? She had told me hundreds of times and must have been expecting me to remember that at least, but I was so careless. I tried her number nearly 20 times and every time it was busy as if she was the first lady in the universe to be so busy.

I tried sending some loving messages but they did not work as there was no reply from her side.

There was a call and it was from my brother, Shahid.

"Hi, bro!"

"Hi Aditya! You were not sleeping, I guess?"

"No! No! I'm for you anytime, bro. Is there anything important?"

"Hey, do you remember talking me once that the wind flowing past when a train moves can be used to generate electricity just as we use the concept of the windmill?"

"Yeah, I remember it." (I had given him thousands of such ideas but an idler like me could never get down to experimenting on it while he loved to work on my ideas.)

"It has been approved by our teacher for the state-level exhibition on 11th. So we have to work it out today as I am leaving for Mussoorie tomorrow morning."

"You mean a night out?"

"Yep! See you at my place at 10 p.m."

"Okay!"

That was friendship. The useless teachers could never entertain your ideas but loved to push down your throat only those ideas that were given in books. Originality and creativity of ideas was not their cup of tea. All they wanted was to make you adjust to their plans.

The whole day I spent walking in my room, thinking how I could make her happy on her birthday. I did not know why I was thinking of her? Maybe because she was a good friend of mine or was it that I loved her? Why was she expecting something from my side? Why did it make her angry that I had not remembered her birthday? Why? These questions kept on bothering my mind.

I took out a card out of my drawer and put it in my bag along with some books to show to my brother. I left my place at 9:30 without taking dinner, expecting to eat a Maggi treat at his place. I walked on the road, thinking about her (whenever I walk on the road, my mind is never with me. It is always lost either in looking at her or working on some ideas that are stored in the primary storage area of my brain.) This time I was pondering upon another extraordinary talent and skill – Aprajita. After some time, my *ulta dimaag* provided me some boost and in the next three minutes I composed a beautiful message to send on my cell-phone.

Who the hell has said that only two human bombs were used? A third was used on August 9, 1989 and it was bound to reveal the disastrous effects just when the clock struck 12. So be ready for the blast as it will reincarnate the cute Aprajita in you. Keep it with care because...

Creativity to the fore...

God said, "Sorry" as Walt Disney is no more alive to create any other cartoon......

Yeah, it worked (my *ulta dimaag* is really great) and I received a call from her. "That's really cute," she said in an enticing voice.

"Thank you, madam," I replied generously.

"So, you are an artist with a fine sense of humour."

"Anything for you, madam," I said, bending in front of the phone.

"What were you doing all this day apart from writing this extraordinarily indelible piece that can floor any girl?"

"Nothing princess; exactly nothing."

"Must be going for your beauty sleep as you have to look great tomorrow," she said naughtily.

"Excuse me madam, boys are hard and tough as I am on my way to Shahid's place for a night out. You must take care of your beauty sleep till your relatives wake you up at 12 o'clock."

"There's no one to wake me up."

"What?" I squealed (I couldn't control my emotions.)

"Yep, my parents are out of the city; gone to a wedding and *Bhai* has some project work to do in college. I don't think he will be coming home this weekend."

"By what time will they be back?" I asked curiously.

"May be two or three."

"Enjoy your lonely birthday."

"You must not forget my birthday this time," she said in a taunting voice and put the phone down.

I liked her attitude; I liked her; I liked her from head to toe. She indeed was so different.

On reaching Shahid's place, I found him blabbering about the project which he had planned out and decided how to implement it at the national level. He told me that the minimum speed of a train required was 100km/hr to generate sufficient amounts of electricity. He had set the track for the train to move on and all we needed was to adjust the batteries at their rightful places to help in moving the turbine for electricity to be produced. I seemed completely at sea during this talk when he angrily asked, "What's wrong with you?"

"I am in love," I said with stars in my eyes.

"So, at last you have had to admit it," he said casually.

"Aren't you excited?" I asked angrily.

"I knew of it all along."

"You are my bro! Shahid, listen, tomorrow is her birthday and she is all alone at her place tonight."

"And mister, how do you know it all?" he asked obliquely.

"She told me."

"Crap! This means she likes you."

"No *yaar*, there is nothing like that. She is just expecting something special from me."

"Okay, you don't believe me. Just rush to her place and see if she allows you inside or not. I will be happy to donate my friend to such a nice girl and heaven forbid, if she does not allow you inside, then just come back to my place. I will find you a bevy of girls to flirt with."

"If you were in her place, would you have allowed me inside?" I asked. (How silly was I to ask him such an idiotic question? But then he was my bro who would have understood the situation.)

"Aditya, don't forget I'm a boy."

"What shall I gift her?"

"Just rush! It is 11:30. You are offering yourself as her boyfriend. The formal rituals can be performed later on" (and he pushed me out of his room, handing me the key to the main door).

I scooted out of his house (it was an easy job as his parents were asleep) and started running. The silent roads seemed always special but this time I had a reason to fly over them, beating the pace of time. The empty roads with their permanent guests prowling around, subjected me to withstand their barking.

They followed me for some time as I had disturbed them from their sleep (anyone on getting disturbed tends to puke out something, while here they were merely stray dogs). The street lights, the closed shutters of the shops seemed to be gazing at me – one who had drifted in front of them without caring for what was happening around. I knew that even if one of the dogs was to bite me, I would not have stopped, come what may. With all what I had in my power, I wanted to make the day a special one for her. I wanted to give her a card.

I managed to reach her place by 11:55 and found a lock hanging on the bolt outside her house. I tried her number desperately, but she did not pick up. I stood, looking confused and sweating profusely. I kept pondering over the situation before concluding that she might have fallen asleep and her parents could have locked the house from outside as she was all alone. Without forcing my brain to analyse the situation, I did what my heart urged me to do – I entered her house like an intruder crossing the six-foot-high wall (Thank God, no one had spotted me). Just as I placed my foot in her house, my phone rang, displaying the name of my princess who lived in this palace, which I had just now entered illegally.

"Sorry! I..." she began to stammer.

"Happy birthday, princess!"

"Thank you!" she replied generously.

"So, what is the plan?"

"Just plan to get my beauty sleep."

"Wait! Wait! Can you please come out in the garden?"

"Why?"

"I have left a gift for you there. Please collect that. I always wanted to make it special, but all I could manage was this gift. I hope you would like it!"

She took nearly two minutes to come out and her instant reaction was, "Gee! how could you manage it all at such short notice?" she asked, blushing with embarrassment.

I did it, finally...

She invited me inside her room. (Shahid was right – she liked me, else she would not have invited me inside.)

I wanted to praise her for looking so dazzlingly beautiful in a simple night-suit. It could be because she had not worn any thing else under her top. Yes, she had worn a sky-blue-coloured top with a big picture of Winnie the Pooh adorning the front, while short pyjamas covered her sexy legs. Her wet hair kept flying across her cheeks. Evidently she had just taken a bath and her face gleamed brightly, her lips looked a moist pink and her small feet looked so dainty. I just wanted to kiss her as she looked simply awesome. I was convinced that she was some witch to be able to drive me crazy. The mind-blowing beauty standing in front of my eyes made me wonder how such a beauty could take a liking to an idiot like me?

I was happy that I could see her in her lovely night-suit which displayed her sexy figure to the hilt, increasing my love for her. I considered myself unusually lucky to be able to see her looking the most sexiest. Her ineluctable beauty had cast a spell on me and the delicious fragrance from her body simply knocked my senses out. I stood in front of her, breathing with difficulty while stammering what I had come prepared to say. I tried to form more words to say to her but my lips moved though no sound emanated from them. Finally with immense difficulty, I managed to say something, though most of it must have been quite incomprehensible to her. "I...I..am simply struck dumb!" I uttered.

"But why?" she asked innocently. (Gosh, her voice sounded no less sexy than her looks.)

"The lock outside your house and with you not picking up the phone made me frantic."

"Aditya (my name sounded so nice when her lips uttered them), my parents left at 8 o'clock, so they locked the house from outside for my security. When you called, I was taking my bath."

"So I can see," I said, understanding the situation.

"What do you understand?" she squeaked.

"Promise me, you won't get upset," I said, returning to my senses.

"I promise!" she said with a smile playing on her lips.

"You are looking devastatingly beautiful. You are looking sweet sixteen while I feel like a four-year child muttering all this to you. My brain has ceased to work. Whatever I have spoken is cent per cent truth coming directly from my heart," I said in a single breath. I do not know how I could say it all.

"Thank you, *chhota baccha*, but let me tell you that you are *besharam* to enter my house like an intruder at midnight. Nevertheless, I appreciate your *besharmi*," she said with her eyes twinkling.

"So what's up now?" she asked.

"Nothing!" I said.

"I think there is nothing to eat and I don't know cooking either," she admitted sorrowfully. (Her smile was the greatest weapon ever. I am sure if any girl were to ask me to jump from the Himalayas with Aprajita's kind of smile on her face, I would have definitely taken the plunge without even thinking that I needed first to climb it before jumping from there.)

"Hey! Do you have 'Maggi'?" I asked all of a sudden, hoping to impress her with my culinary skill.

"Yup! I love it. That must surely be there in the kitchen."

"Let's raid your kitchen," I suggested. (A night out with Shahid had at least taught me to cook 'Maggi' noodles efficiently)

I prepared the noodles while she kept staring at what all I was doing with a look of curiosity that is seen in a three-year old child. She was simply unbearably cute. With the increasing heat of the boiling water, my body temperature was rising slowly and steadily to burst my senses. I felt like the 'Maggi' in the pan, lost in the sea of love with a partner who could bring taste to my life. God, the rising heat and the boiling water were ready to chalk out my destiny. She helped by handing me a service-spoon on a plate, when quite inadvertently my hand touched hers, sending an electric current through my body and making my senses reel with confusion. At long last the 'Maggi' was ready and so were we to pounce upon it with full gusto.

Sitting in her room, we ate the 'Maggi' with the solitary service spoon and in the same saucepan used for cooking, since we did not want to bother with washing any extra utensils. I was supposed to be the one to wash the utensils as I doubted if she could have ever washed the dishes in her life. So as soon as we had eaten, I turned to washing the utensils. She kept standing at my side and when I finished, all of a sudden, she planted a kiss of gratitude on my left cheek. She cooed, "I love you, *besharam* cook." We both proceeded to her room where she asked for her gift. I fell to my knees and with a flourish took out the card from behind my back (hidden between my T-shirt and casuals). Smilingly I handed the card to her and said, "This is only for my princess."

She was completely taken aback at the card and asked, "What is this?" (How could I blame her for her genuine question when I handed her a card on her birthday at midnight and that too which was neither a birthday card nor a Valentine card).

She read it out loudly:

Ms & Mr Relhan
request the pleasure of your benevolent blessings and
seek your eminent presence to share our joy at the
delightful occasion of the wedlock of their only son

Aditya
With

"Crap! What's all this?" she asked, looking perplexed.

"I'm proposing to you Aprajita," I said.

"Are you out of your mind or something?"

"No, *yaar*, I feel you are the only one for me. Actually, since my childhood I have been excited about making my own wedding card and this I am offering you, leaving the lower portion blank for you to fill up the rest with your name and a line for the great people who have given you birth. I want to capture this auspicious moment of my life on this piece of paper, so that I can always remember our beautiful relationship. I also invite you as my future wife to our wedding. As you are the most important aspect of this invitation, I want to offer this card first of all to you."

"Am I the first one to get this card?" she asked.

"No, I started it all when I was in the nursery. I gave one to the one who took the card home. I was quite certain that she would not be knowing how to spell her name, but the next day, she came to school with her Dad. I tried this same act with Gabby, who again turned my cheeks red. On both occasions my cards were torn off ruthlessly. However, you are the first girl in front of whom I have offered my card by bending down on my knees."

"Hey, what is it that could make me blind?"

"Dear princess, they say that love is blind but I would say that the one who is actually in love is blind. I can see the image of only one and luckily for me, I have found that image in you. So, please allow my eyes to get lost in your beauty and be the lucky blind."

She took it and filled it with that lovely name of hers – Aprajita D/O Mrs & Mr Khanna. I felt I was flying in seventh heaven as now she was willing to be mine and only mine. She handed back the card to me, saying, "Now, I want it back on the most important day of our life. It is my future gift but where is my present gift? I am born just today."

I thought for a second and then spotted the mirror. I made her look into the mirror before asking, "What do you see in the mirror?"

"Me!" she said very innocently.

"It is not just you; it is the noble gift that God has awarded this earth on this very date to fulfil life for people like me, with whom your destiny is tied and I find nothing more interesting than you to gift you," I said and planted a kiss on the black spot below her lips before adding, "I love you, Aprajita."

She turned and reciprocated by kissing me on my lips. I clutched her tightly in my arms, placing one hand across her waist and the other sliding across her neck to touch her wet hair. I nibbled at her ear playfully and again we kissed. I started licking her lips, her cheeks, playing with her wet hair and slipping one hand inside her top. Oh how soft was her skin! I felt I was going mad. Just as my hand reached her boobs inside her top, my phone vibrated (she had already turned her phone off). It was bloody Shahid (when I was on my way to reach the zenith of my greatest experience, he had interrupted).

"Aditya, it's already 1:45 and you must come back, bro. It is getting late and her parents will be back soon," he said, sounding worried.

I turned to her (oh, she looked more alluring after the kiss, her seductive looks serving as a hurdle to my departure from her place), "Okay Aprajita, it is getting late. I must leave now."

She said, "I love you, *besharam*" and pulled me towards her again (that was the power of love when you are at the mercy of your partner), our lips just a few millimetres away. She tilted her head sideways (I did what she wanted, despite being the defeated one) and again we kissed, (my body temperature rising infinitely and my senses reeling. I could not resist licking her lips, pressing her boobs, sliding my hand on her cuddly skin at her back and getting more and more excited and energetic. She began to kiss my face, my neck wildly and my hand pulled her T-shirt below her shoulder as I found kissing her sides greater fun. I could feel her skin turn more and more soft and seductive as my one hand crept to her breast and the other slid behind her back. Again my cell vibrated, startling us from the tight embrace we were caught in. It was Shahid again, who said, "It is 2 o'clock, bro!"

"Love you, princess," I murmured into her ears, before turning to leave.

She replied innocently, "Love you too Hardy Boy."

"What's that?" I queried.

"That's your new name from today."

She looked ravishingly beautiful after the kiss and her skin glowed pink, possibly from the onslaught of my hands. That's how our love story started, crossing the phase of longing. Now the problem was her parents who were still in the dark about our affair and because of whom, I dare not approach her whenever I wanted.

An unusual call...

October 2, 2009 (09:00)

A call arrived from Dodo, one of my friends who I considered an imbecile. "Why the fuck have you called me at 9 in the morning?" I shouted at him.

"Shahid is dead," he said and began to howl.

"Shut up, you jerk. I am not in the mood for jokes at this early hour." I screamed at him.

He began to cry loudly and mumble, "I am sorry to tell you Aditya, but it is true. I have the bloody paper in my hands. Yesterday night (he began to stammer as he could not speak coherently) Bike No. 1881 was struck by a drunken truck-driver, killing Shahid on the spot."

"Just keep your bloody mouth shut, Dodo. This is not my idea of fun. Tell me that you are joking. Say it *nah*, please Dodo," I begged, tears rolling down my cheeks.

"I'm not joking, bastard. Just check out today's newspaper..." sobbing and muttering in turn.

"Tell me you are joking," I shouted, but he put the phone down as he could no continue any further.

When I looked at my phone to check whether it was Dodo or someone else, I noticed 18 missed calls from Shahid's Mom. I was completely at a loss, not knowing what to do or say, I wanted to give vent to my anger upon myself, 'Oh, why did I keep my phone on vibration mode?' The bloody phone sucked. I threw the phone away with anger, 'Why could it not wake me up on time when required?'

Crap, the bloody phone lay broken into tiny pieces.

My mind started working and thinking, 'There must be something wrong with Shahid because he could not have died all of a sudden. He was my best bastard friend; he just could not die, leaving me all alone behind like this. Shahid just die.'

I dashed to my car and rushed towards Shahid's place. On reaching the house, I could not believe what my eyes saw. I hated my eyes for seeing what they did. My eyes were revealing all that they were seeing. Why were my eyes so loyal to me? Why didn't they have the brain to let me see only what my heart wanted to see and not anything else? I felt helpless and lost as if the world had come crashing down. Why had God been so cruel as to kill my friend, my bro? Why had God taken my friend instead of me? I hated everything and everyone and found the world the most despicable place to live in.

My eyes noticed a crowd of people seated, dressed in white *kurtas*, white sarees, white suits, and white everything. But why white? White is considered the colour of peace but here was the place where the rocking Shahid lived, always full of life and clamour. Why were all of them gathered here? I simply could not take it. No, Aditya, no, it could not be true! Everything was going to be alright. I had noticed that adversities never knock on your door by announcing their arrival. They come all of a sudden to rob you of your happiness, your peace, your satisfaction. It was the most horrific sight and most atrocious moment of my life to see the crowd gathered and the body of my brother lying on the floor. Life was really a tough game with no rules laid or followed. (Had it been possible, I would have asked God to make Shahid immortal.) The body of my brother lay in front of my eyes, but he was not aware of me.

It was then that I realised why some relationships are above blood relations because they develop for no reason. They strengthen your belief and make you live each and every moment of your life. You can share with such relations whatever you want to tell and they would never tell. They would even be prepared to die for you, if required. They would cheer you at your success without caring about their own sorrows. They would willingly walk hand-in-hand with you at each step of your life, without expecting anything in return. They would always be prepared to tell you that there was nothing to fear so long as they were at your side. They are the ones who would promise even to battle Yamraj if he ever came to get you and that is what Shahid meant to me. He was dead; he was no longer alive. He used to say, "*Din woh bhi nahi rahenge, na din ye bhi nahi rahenge, isse bekaar bhi abhi aane hai*" Yes, he was absolutely right (this is the worst of all) but from where would I get a friend like him ever again?

His body lay numb and listless and I felt as if I too had become dumb and listless. I sat there numb, dumbly looking around. I noticed his mother mourning the loss of her only child and sitting surrounded by her neighbours and relatives, all of whom were trying to console her. His father stood in front of his son's photograph, staring at it but without blinking his eyes and letting tears flow down of their own volition. His cousins were engaged in a heated discussion with the police. Watching all this, a tear dropped from my eye and I screamed, "Get up, you bastard. Let the game end now, Shahid. If you continue this way, I won't talk to you for the rest of my life." I was not aware of what I was saying. Vibhor, Gabby and Pumpi tried to pull me away (we were together after a long period because after school, all your friends tend to disperse and form new groups). Shahid was the only one who was missing from my group. Could it be that he was upset with me? I just wanted to close my eyes to confirm that what I was seeing was happening in a bloody dream. The day had not started yet, and it was still 1st of October.

I thought that possibly if I closed my eyes, everything that I was seeing in front of my eyes would vanish and I would return to earth. But reality can never be wiped away. You have to live with it, like it or not. This horrendous reality had robbed me of my friend, my brother, my confidant, my hero, my life, my world. The most promising student of our batch, my Shahid, was no more!

No more would there ever be those happy times that we had spent together; no more would there be those back-breaking projects, which we had messed up together a number of times; no more would there be any night outs when we could kill our time; no more would there be our 'Maggi' dinners; no more would there be a friend in need and deed. No more! No more!

Why could I not just stop time and rewind it to get rid of this traumatic incident in my life? Why could I not escape it? I felt so helpless, so impotent, so useless! Oh God, how could I just sit and watch my brother lie dead? What could I do to bring him back to life?

I kept sitting there, numb with shock and hearing people discuss how his bike had been struck down by a drunken truck-driver, who had mowed him to death. Oh God, why did Shahid have to go out on his bike at night? Why? Did he not know that it was dangerous? No, he did not for why would he have driven at night? He was a fool, an idiot to burn his petrol at night for no possible reason.

I began to hate all those who drink, especially those bloody rascals who drive after getting drunk. I was ready to kill all those bastards in just one go. It was one such bastard who had snatched my brother from me. I could kill them all.

I felt as if I was dead in body, dead in my senses and dead to the world around me. I could not erase memories of Shahid from my mind and his face kept on cropping up in front of my eyes. Shahid's father asked me to give a hand in carrying dear Shahid's pier and I felt as if I had been ordered to carry my own corpse. I felt I was participating in my own funeral and moving like a robot. They began to chant, "*Ram naam satya hai*" but try as I would, I could not utter a single word. How could I do it when my soul, my brother had gone to meet the universal soul?

I felt it was my corpse that was being carried to the cremation ground and that I was following to be burnt and to die and disappear forever.

I really did die on that cremation ground. I really did die in the funeral ceremony of my brother.

I really had died when the words "*Ram naam satya hai*" were being chanted.

I really had died with all those crying voices that filled his house.

I really had died in that accident.

I had died! I was dead!

The rituals kept me bound the whole day and I did not know how to face his parents or how to face my parents or how to face this world. I wished I too had physically died with Shahid. I would have to live but without my soul.

I rushed to my place and kept walking up and down, remembering the wonderful moments that we had spent together. I could see Shahid smiling sometimes, crying sometimes, groaning sometimes and getting lost sometimes in the cycle of life. The bloody bastard had left me midway without allowing me to laugh for some more time at least. He had robbed me of all happiness, leaving me behind all alone to fend for myself. Now there would be no one to ring me up and say, "*Saale*, don't you see my bloody face around you all the day that you want me to come now also?"

I kept waiting for his phone call but none came as he was no longer there. Now who would help me to kill time? I took out a piece of paper and began to write, as tears flowed like a stream from my eyes.

Tears...
Yes, tears rolled down my cheeks,
signifying my life fallen from a peak.
They carried all the fears I had in my mind
symbolising a downward sign.
I gave 'them' birth, but you weren't there to nurture
without taking leave from my eye,
they flowed under the laws of Nature.
They seemed to move only on the surface
but deep somewhere they had shaken
my each and every corner of life
to flow down and flow and flow endlessly,
to tell stories that are untold.
Resistance to their motion describes
I am still bold.
They show how I am so helpless,
searching for a gate to confess.
They are scolding the world in an inaudible voice
They represent my crying heart without any noise.

I still cannot believe that Shahid is dead. We had a planned to watch the movie "Wake up Sid", although he had narrated the whole script beforehand. I still believe that I am lost in sleep and that when I open my eyes, everything would vanish away. I would open my eyes to a new morning and Shahid's death would be just one nightmare that would vanish away. It had to be some atrocious dream. I looked at the clock and noticed it was 3 o'clock, time for him to make me a call. He had the stupid habit of waking people up at such an ungodly hour. I knew he would call me. I just had to wait for his call. But there was no call. This was the reality and I was a bloody loser, who could do nothing. I started to cry, banging my head against the wall, hitting my fists on my bed, tearing off my personal diary that described all the wonderful experiments conducted by us. I began to sob uncontrollably as everything that I had once treasured would no longer hear my voice. I tried to avoid the things that reminded me of Shahid, but unfortunately my room, everything around me, even my own body could not stop me from remembering this selfish friend. I was left on earth only to cry and cry....

When I dozed off on my bed after a long bout of tears, I decided to talk to Aprajita, who was evidently unaware of this mishap for if she had known, she would have definitely called me up. I needed a shoulder to cry on; I needed some-one. I could not cry in front of my parents as I did not want to increase their sorrow. Shahid meant more than me to them as he was first their son and later my friend.

Crap! I had to tell all this to Aprajita.

I suddenly remembered that it was her parents' silver wedding anniversary. How times had changed. Only yesterday we had been discussing the occasion to come but when it had arrived, I did not know how to receive it. I think this is what is life – it changes every few seconds.

I must call her. Crap, where has the phone gone? Oh yes, I had broken my phone into pieces which were lying in the corner of my room. I took out the SIM card and inserted it into the other mobile phone. I waited for a few minutes and noticed 30 new messages, all from my friends who were reminding me of the harsh reality, which I was trying to escape at any cost. I knew I could not run away from the reality, try as I might. I was a loser. It was not my fault; it was my heart, which was looking at the world with new eyes.

I did not want to read any message; I just wanted to talk to Aprajita, but she was not picking up the phone. She must be asleep as it was quite late. I desperately wanted to talk to her as the sorrow engulfing me was drowning me into a deep abyss from which I wanted to save myself.

I tried her number again and again, but she did not pick up. I wanted to tell her that she was the only one who could offer support to me in my condition. Then I messaged her (my hands were trembling with fear while typing the message and tears kept rolling down at a feverish pace). Finally I messaged her, "Shahid is dead."

I dozed off on my bed, crying, smiling, groaning, howling and waiting for his call. I knew Shahid could not live without talking to me for a single day. I kept lying on my bed, my eyes focused on the phone in the hope of receiving a call from him. I did not know when I fell asleep.

The next morning I got up, hoping to forget everything about Shahid but the world is not so considerate as to allow anyone to escape the reality so easily. My phone was filled with messages of commiseration from my bloody friends and with dozens of missed calls. I knew they wanted to sympathise with me, but what was the use? They could not bring my friend back to this earth. They could only remind me that my soul was dead. I became exasperated at all of them for being unable to help me. Why could I not wipe away this phase of my life? Why had no elixir been found, despite all the advancements in science and technology to the extent that man had even set foot on the Moon? How could God be so cruel? Why was he like this?

Unfortunately some questions are never answered. My mind wanted to shout out loudly but it could only echo my words: 'I don't want to go out in this world without my bro. I don't want to do anything; I just want to keep sitting and recollect all those merry moments we had spent together; the memories that I had stored somewhere deep in my heart. I just wanted Shahid. I wanted to see him and go to his lair. I kept sitting in one place, looking vacantly into space and wishing Shahid to appear from somewhere. My ears longed to hear his voice just once; my hands moved to shake hands with him for the last time; my brain kept on reminiscing about the places where we could go to be away from the madding crowd. I was really going out of my mind. I was turning into a misanthrope; I had gone completely mad. Had I? In order to forget the reality I wanted to escape somewhere which would not remind me of him. I did not want to live. I wanted to quit.

My Mom was busy with her routine work but was silent working like a machine. She was the one who loved to talk to me whenever I returned home on weekends. Silence was a stranger to the house. I knew that deep within her heart she was missing her son. He was her life and I just could not bring myself to face her. Facing the world was now bound to become pretty irksome.

I needed Aprajita to talk to. I called her, but she was not picking the phone. It kept on ringing and ringing. I put the phone down hastily.

A few hours later, I noticed it was her call. "Hi Aditya!" she said in a low tone.

"Hi!" I replied heavily.

"I'm sorry about Shahid," she began to cry. (I know girls are somewhat more emotional than boys. They can never prevent the flow of tears from their eyes.)

Shahid was a good friend of hers too. She could not even get a last glimpse of him. I remained silent while she kept on sobbing. I wanted to console her but how could I when I myself was going through hell? I wanted to say something but did not know what to say. Aprajita however was brave enough to continue, "I am sorry, but we can't do anything about it. The law of life is that life goes on, no matter how much we suffer. So, just keep moving; problems will come and go. The show must go on. Remember, between every difficulty lies an opportunity," she said in a low tone.

"Is Shahid's death just another problem for you?" I screamed.

"No Aditya, but try to understand," she said.

"I don't know how to react. I have completely lost my mind," I said.

"Look, everything will be alright. We just need to cross this tough patch in our life," she said, regaining her lost voice.

"Hope so! I want to meet you. I want a shoulder to cry on. My tears are waiting to pour out of my eyes but there is no one to offer me solace. I simply need you, Aprajita. I am caught in this hopeless situation where things seem dark and eerie. This silence will kill me. I need you because there is no one else who can understand me. I need you," I said, bursting into tears.

"No," she replied instantly.

"Please, I am dying to meet you."

"No, Aditya."

"Please! I beg of..." I began to cry like a three-year old child. "But why not?" I asked.

"Mom is not well."

"What's wrong with her?" I was surprised to hear about this new development.

I heard a loud voice call out to Aprajita by her name ...

"She is calling me; need to rush. 'Bye!" she said, placing the phone down without wasting a second.

"Jesus, can't she spare even a few minutes for me? Is she so busy that she can't talk to me properly? I need her desperately. I need her."

I tried her number again and again, But each time she cut my call and I grew tired of hearing the recorded voice say, "The number you are trying to reach is currently busy."

After an hour, I received a message from her, 'Mom is suffering from high fever and cannot be left alone. Sorry, cannot talk to you. Hope you will understand.'

Yeah, why not? She expected me to understand her problem but had no time to understand mine? I replied to her message: 'Can we meet? Please! Any place near your home, just for half an hour.'

And she replied instantly, 'No! I cannot.'

She was not even prepared to spare a mere 30 minutes for her boyfriend, who was passing through a traumatic situation. I wrote on the outbox section of my cell phone the following message: 'Plz!' but she reciprocated on the inbox section with the reply. 'No!'

I, however, did not give up hope. I decided to wait for her call, hoping that she would change her mind. Her reasons sounded just untenable. If her mother was not well, she must be resting or sleeping, when Aprajita could actually come out. She was behaving in an unusually callous manner. Earlier, she could find time to spare from her busy schedule just to gaze at my face but today, when I needed her desperately, she was not willing to spare a few minutes. Earlier she would tell her Mom a lie just to meet me, but now she had changed.

Finally I messaged her: 'Just give me a call the moment you are free', but no reply came. I tried her number again and again but no response was forthcoming. Finally I gave up in disgust. I just hated her. Not only did she begin to disconnect my calls, she even ceased to reply to my messages. At the end I compromised with the situation and put my phone down.

My day was spent in routine activities, which were essential for my body to survive – food, walk, sleep but something was missing somewhere down the road. I was dying to hear Shahid's giggle, his silly pranks and his funky messages. The day put extra pressure on me as the difficult task ahead of me meant somehow ignoring the calls of my bastard friends.

At 11 p.m. I tried her number, but she cut my calls every time that I tried. Some time later, I received a message from her and the rest of our conversation was through messages:

'Dear, I'm really tired taking care of Mom this whole day. Can't talk to you; sleeping with Mom.'

'Is she critical?'

'No, just high fever. Doctors have recommended complete bed-rest.'

'Can we meet tomorrow?'

'No!'

'I desperately need to talk to you. I am losing control over my senses. I don't care how you do it, but we have to meet tomorrow at Share Cafe at 11 in the morning.'

'I am sorry, it won't be possible.'

'You have to be there, *jaanu*!'

'No, I cannot.'

'If you love me, then you have to.'

'No. Try to understand, it is impossible to leave her alone.'

She continued refusing but I did not pay any heed to her messages. I wanted to meet her and when you are close to each other, you have the right to put pressure on your partner. If you need their help, you need not ask them. You can simply order them and expect them to be by your side. You have the option to ask for a shoulder to cry on, or the support of the partner's arms to embrace you at a time when you require a hug, or words of appreciation to let you know that you are strong enough to overcome your problem. After all, it is your partner who can make you realise the reason of your living as he or she is the one whom you really love.

Next day, I reached the cafe half an hour before the scheduled time to sit and wait for her arrival. I began to recall the past occasions when she really supported me, making our relationship special, the times when she was the only one to support me, and the times when I felt she was the only one for me. It is said that after entering into a relationship, one gets drawn away from friends and family, but this is wrong. It was not she who ever stood in the way of my attending to my social obligations. If Shahid and I ever got into a fight and neither of us was willing to relent, it was she who, like a true princess, came in between to help us solve our argument. She would often invite us individually without revealing her plan and find out what troubled either of us and then suggest a solution. It was she who often told us, "If you know that the other person is a good friend of yours, do not let any misunderstanding spoil your relationship and remember boys, it is always your male friends who can really help you out." She had always been a guide to me and helped me develop a positive attitude towards life and society. She could make me laugh even in the most harrowing situations of life.

She was the one who helped me choose between science and commerce. I wanted to pursue commerce as I thought it would be an easy subject to handle and I could get time to enjoy life. But it was she who said that science would help me in taking a line where there would be greater openings for future employment. She had said that even if it meant going far from her, it was nothing big because distances did not affect relationships; instead they helped to boost the bonding in the relationship. Yes, she had proved right as our relationship had strengthened after that.

She gave support even in my personal life when after my sister's marriage, I became very lonely and worried that my sister would have to face problems in adjusting to a strange place and strange people, but Aprajita made me realise that girls are strong enough to cope up with new situations when the need arises. What is more, on my parent's silver wedding anniversary, while I had planned on giving a surprise party outside the house, she instead suggested sending my parents out for a movie and then preparing dinner for them myself. Although she herself was a stranger to the kitchen, she had personally downloaded all the recipes from the Internet to get me to cook. She voluntarily prepared a photo-album, placing the photographs beginning from the time of their marriage to the present life, including writing out emotional captions below each photograph. On seeing this, my parents' eyes filled with tears as they were deeply touched at the effort put in.

After entering into a relationship with her, I wasn't very sure if she was the right one for me, but one day, while talking about our relationship, she said to me, "Aditya, you've always taken me as an option but I don't know why I love you still?" I had become terribly embarrassed at her observation because it was the truth and I could not help admiring her for a mature head on such young shoulders. From that day onwards I came to accept that she was the only one for me and that I really loved her.

She glittered like a gem in my life and always supported me right from the front, serving as a friend, as a mentor and as a confidant.

Coming back to the present, I realised that a lot of time had passed but there was no sign of her. I tried to call her number, but her cell was switched off. I tried it again and again till my wristwatch revealed that it was 2:30 now. Finally I left the place without having coffee, but without losing hope that she would call me any time. Despite calling her a number of times, I continued receiving the same message: 'The number you're trying to call is currently switched off.'

I was highly infuriated with her insensitive action.

I kept on trying her number all day long (I did not have anything else to do and I had become addicted to hearing her voice), but her cell had been switched off. Finally in exasperation, I sent the message: 'Just give me a call,'

Shockingly enough, there was no call from her. For the next two days I kept on trying her number and receiving the same response. I sent her the message: 'I am worried for her. I hope it is nothing serious!' I needed to know the exact situation. I called her best friend Arushi, who was a complete flirt and her beauty added to her devious nature.

"Hi Arushi! How are you?"

"I am great. What's up Aditya?"

"Cool *yaar*! Where are you?"

"Shimla!"

"Sorry!"

"At Shimla, watching the boys saunter up and down the Mall as I am still single after you ditched me for Aprajita," she said.

"Shut up! How can you be in Shimla?"

"Dumbo, didn't anybody inform you about our 10-day tour to Shimla, Kufri and all? Aprajita must have told you surely, lover boy. I still wonder if I could ever get to know a boy like you in my life."

"Yep, she told me." (In fact, she had told me and expressed her inability to accompany them, possibly because her mother was seriously ill.)

While I was thinking of this, Arushi said, "Do not worry, darling, I'll be there on 13th, so that we can again go dating. But this time we will not tell Aprajita about it because she will kill you if she gets to know of it, my sweet little boy."

"Yeah, why not?"

"You tell me why you have called your long lost girlfriend?"

"How is Aprajita?"

"Come again! I can't believe my ears. Are you Aditya, her boyfriend? If you have broken up with her, please let me know. I will be willing to replace her."

"Actually, her phone has been switched off since the past three days and her mother is not well too."

"Hey! Being possessive."

"No, just concerned."

"I talked to her this morning only. Her phone has gone dead because in anger, she tossed it down many times on the floor. That is why her number is not working. Her mother is lying in bed, suffering from fever and Aprajita is concerned and upset about her."

"Wait, was she not supposed to go on a tour?"

"Yep, but she backed out at the last moment when she found her mother feeling unwell."

"Thanks, Arushi."

"Anytime, dude. I am all yours, but tell me one thing, are you alright?"

"Yeah! Why are you asking?"

"Because you are sounding somewhat different; somewhat subdued. Promise that you are not lying?"

"Promise, *yaar*. Do not get sentimental."

"Then promise me that you will leave Aprajita for me!"

"Yeah, sure, any time."

"Stop flirting, just take care of your relationship, you lover."

"Okay, ask her to call me if she calls you next."

"Yeah, I will do that."

Thank God, everything was fine but why could she not call me since the past two days?

At last, her call...

October 9, 2009

"Hi Aditya!" she greted very sweetly.

"Hi! Where have you been all these days?"

"Hey *jaanu*, Mom wasn't well. I was quite busy taking care of her."

"So, is she dead now that you have found time to call?"

"Shut up, Aditya. Are you conscious of what you are saying?"

"I am sorry. I am deeply disturbed."

"Okay Aditya, but please get over Shahid. A whole life lies in front of you and these problems will accompany you for the rest of your life. Does it mean you will just sit at one place and keep mourning day and night?"

"Okay, I will try to get over it," I replied in a pensive mood.

"Why are you sounding so depressed?" she screamed.

"Stop talking like a nun and please do not compel me to say something undiplomatic," I said.

"What? Just tell what you actually want to say."

"No, Aprajita, you won't feel good on hearing what I have in mind."

"Please Aditya, go ahead."

"Well you are seated at home since the past one week with an inexcusable reason that your Mom is not well and espousing great philosophies. Do you even know the pain of losing someone? Thank God, your Mom suffered only from a mild fever. I wonder what would have happened if she were to get hospitalised, or lost her kidneys, or suffered a heart attack or something like that! I suppose you would have definitely died out of sorrow and pain. I can gange if something wrong were to transpire with your family, you would not be able to bear it, you baby."

I put the phone down, cursing her and calling her a bitch. Pumpi had been right when she had referred to Aprajita as being studious. She knew only what the books said but nothing about the practical world, which is quite different from bookish knowledge. She knew how to subscribe to the crazy philosophy that you have to move on, come what may. She could lecture on all her bloody philosophies and come to terms with the reality. She knew how to resort to rhetoric but when it came to the practical aspect, she was all at a loss for words.

I concluded that after all, love was only trash. During the periods of happiness, she was present to hold my hand but when the time came when I needed help, she started avoiding me. She could not even spare a few minutes from her busy schedule. Surely her mother could not be requiring baby-feeding! How could she be so insensitive? Here I have lost my brother, but she was hardly concerned. She had no idea how much pain I was going through on losing my loved brother, my loved one, who was so special, so dear and so close to my heart. She did not love me; she loved only her family, especially her desperate Mom. She could not find a few minutes to be with me. How would she ever stand by my side during the ups and downs of life? Thank God, I discovered this well on time! It was good that I had come to know how selfish she was. She was proud, impudent and self-centred. I simply hated her. She was a bitch, a minx but how was I live without her? Maybe there was something wrong with her. She was a lovely princess, my Aprajita, with whom I need to talk.

Uncle D, my friend...

Lastly, the only alternative I had was to contact Uncle D. Oh yes, he was the best choice I could think of because he had been with me since the time I was born. He had been my Dad's best friend and had now become an equally great friend of mine and knew me from head to toe.

Uncle D (Drishya Roy) was a charismatic character. In his 40s, he had touched great heights of success. As per his name, he had proved true to his name (*drishya* means 'the vision to see the impossible happen'). He had created his own empire, called Angel Empire right from scratch. His national empire covered all the fields – chemical, IT, cars, telecom, textile and all. His Angel Empire also had a production house sponsoring many blockbuster movies. The company's name was also given to many great banners; it also had some international collaborations in its pocket. His life had been an extraordinary story of success and achievements. I guess if I were to write a book on his life depicting his struggles, a positive attitude and unusual plans, I would take a week because there was nothing to think of. It was all in front of my eyes. Moreover, I respected him a lot, so I was ready to pay a tribute to him any time. Come to think of it, I was willing to even give up my life if he asked for it because I knew that Uncle D was always right. He was my hero, my icon, my God. I just wanted to walk in his shoes.

He was a great friend of mine though I did not know why? Some relations develop due to no rhyme or reason. They have no connection with the selfish or materialistic world. They form to make your life worthwhile and you can find no explanation for their development. Age difference were of no importance when we got together. The generation gap fell to zero when we both entered into a discussion. Life acquired a meaning when I sat next to him because he made me realise that I was important and that there was a huge task lying ahead of me. He was the reason for which I am breathing, the reason for which I am a part of this game called life, the reason for which I have added to the burden on this planet Earth (though I am underweight otherwise). He was inspiring, motivating, lively and yet so calm and sensitive as an innocent child. He was great but I hate God for keeping Uncle D deprived of happiness in life. He has been all alone as his parents died in a car accident and being their only child, he has been left all alone and unmarried. His career has become his life, his wife, his everything since the time he entered the corporate world.

He has been the best person to share my feelings with because he is never judgemental but tries to understand my view on things. I have come to realise that there are some bonds which are so strong that they are formed without any rhyme or reason. All I know is that they are special and strong and that is how I would describe the bond between Uncle D and me.

I called up Uncle D and said excitingly, "Hi Uncle D!"

"Hi dude. What's up? How are all your girl friends?" he shot back (he treated me like his class friend). This was one question he always loved to ask despite knowing the fact that I was committed to one.

"Everybody is waiting for you."

"Truly?"

"Yep!"

"Then tell them to wait more. I really want to meet them all but this business is keeping me tied. However, I promise, I will take out time for all of them."

"Okay, anything else, sir?"

"Is Aprajita one of them?" he asked laughingly (he loved to pull my leg about it whenever he got the chance.)

"She's all yours, sir."

"Okay, then date with her at my place and use all my services. It's all for you Aditya."

"Thanks. I am lucky to have a friend like you who is prepared to take care of all my bills."

"So, tell your financer about your problem, buddy."

"Nothing."

"I know you have a problem, dude."

"How do you know it?" I asked astonishingly.

"I had heard about Shahid from your Dad."

"You know about Shahid?"

"Yep! That's why I was expecting your call since the past one week, but *bachcha*, you are late."

"Sorry Uncle D. Actually I have broken up with Aprajita."

"What?" he literally screamed.

"Not actually but I'm frustrated with her insensible attitude. She is too self-centred...."

He interrupted me, "Wait! Wait! Are you free tomorrow?"

"Yeah, I am at your disposal."

"Great, then rush to my place for a night out and it has been rather long since we last ate 'Maggi' together. This time it is your turn to cook and the BMW X-9 is waiting for you. So, see you at 10:00 o'clock at my place."

"'Bye!"

Thank God, he could spare time for me and also his BMW X-9. Uncle D called me his successor to this car of his and referred to me as the junior driver to all his cars. I am supposed to be the owner of Angel Empire. Night outs with Uncle D were always special affairs as you got to learn a lot and have a lot of fun too. Once we both raced between his two BMW's parked at the end of a one kilometre-long road at 3:00 in the morning and I won that race. Another day, we went for dinner at a *dhabha* and then followed it up by recording videos on the bank of a river at 1:00 in the morning, because he believed that it was the ideal time to record when you are true to yourselves, free of all restrictions, explore as much as you can and do whatever your heart says. That was why we once went to Kasauli just to see the sunrise. He was a lovely person to be with.

Uncle D's place...

Uncle D's house was a place to live in sheer luxury. It was like heaven on earth and because of his liveliness, you could hear his voice all over the place. Most of the walls were adorned with photographs of his parents. There was one photograph of which many copies had been framed in different shapes and sizes that even after watching the original photograph, you felt you were watching something new. You felt as though each and every item was telling a story of how much money and labour must have gone into setting up the Angel Empire. Clippings and notes of articles, published on how the empire was built, the serious problems confronted and the many ups and downs seen to make it what it was now, had been pasted and colour sprayed to make them stand out. Uncle D believed that watching all these reminded him of the times when he was lazy and when energetic, the times when his brain showed how artistic and creative he had been. What was more he had written on the walls (in a very artistic manner) the thoughts and ideas of great and eminent personalities including his own views that spring up in his mind on and off. He had done this so that one day when he would be too old, he could look at them and be reminded of what all he could do when young and full of life. They were like mirrors which reflected not only his image but character too.

You could always find sprayers and syringes at his place and if you wanted to record your thoughts, you were most welcome to do so. You could live life your own way once you set foot on his territory. My favourite was the one he had inscribed in his master bedroom, 'I'm the one yet to be defined' because he believed 'even the last breath that he would take would be meant for a purpose and for that purpose he was the one yet to be defined'. The other thing that I liked most was the phrase he had inscribed, when I had gifted him a novel on his birthday. He had written: 'This is not the best I deserve and not even the best you can give' as he believed that there was no end to success and there was always more to be achieved.

I entered his conference room where different coloured lights could be changed with the click of a button just as any theme can be varied on the mobile phone. He loved changing the colours to suit his moods which was prone to changes and which helped his mind to adjust and think best whatever it wanted to.

He said to me in a serious mood, "So, what's wrong between Aprajita and you?"

Without waiting a second, I blurted out the entire story, presenting a word-by-word picture of all that had transpired between us. After sitting quietly for quite a while and pondering seriously, he said, "Look, Aditya, whatever she said is absolutely correct."

I was surprised to hear his comment and looked askance at him. He explained, "The most important thing in life is to rock to every beat of life and that is your philosophy too, is it not? So what's wrong with it if the music gets sad? I know you are disturbed over Shahid's death but that doesn't mean you should try to run away from reality. Remember, the show must go on."

"But Uncle D, I am really hurt that when my world seems to have collapsed with Shahid's death, my girlfriend seems concerned only about her mother."

"Look, Aditya, in every difficulty there lies an opportunity. So, stop mourning over what has happened and look forward to the opportunity."

"How can I? I'm baffled over all this."

"No you are not. You are just trying to drown in your own sorrow and this way you will not get out of the problem easily. Just open your eyes and look around. The world has not changed. It is still the same ground, the same wind, the same sky. It is time you got up and realised your responsibilities. Now, you have to look after Shahid's parents as well. So, grow up, my boy. Life is same; it is only this that you need to change to be able to adjust."

"But, Aprajita? Why is she doing this to me?"

"Just go to her and discuss out the whole issue. Maybe, something is troubling her mind."

"Are you crazy? You expect me to go to her? Have you gone mad as to tell me to go to her house?"

"Son, you have got to, whether you like it or not."

"Her Hitler-like Dad is always ready to kill me as he does not understand why I breathe on this earth. I am sure he will burn my ass if he were to see me around his house."

"Stop frightening yourself."

"It is, true Uncle D. Her father is a clone of Hitler."

"So, you will never speak to her because you are scared of her Dad?"

"I guess not. I will wait for the right time to come."

"Keep your hand on your heart!" he said politely.

"What?" I squeaked.

"Close your eyes and just do as I say," he said, pointing to my hand and I did as he said.

"Do you love Aprajita?" he asked, his tone turning aggressive.

"Yes! I do." (I could not tell a lie at such a moment when the question was so direct from my uncle.)

"Do you want to talk to her?"

"Yes! I do."

The euphoria of talking to her was taking me to the seventh heaven and I could see all around her face with her characteristic smile which had made me crazy with love for her. Uncle D said in a commanding voice, "Then go and talk to her."

"I find your suggestion inexpedient. Why don't you think over it logically?" I shot back.

"If you love her, think right from the heart and don't let your socially dead brain dominate."

"I love her, that's why I'm thinking of it. One stupid action on my part may land me into a bigger mess than what I am in at the moment. For all you know, I may end up losing her. I don't want anything like that to happen. In fact I had been hoping to spend the rest of my life with her."

"Let your heart do the talking. Allow the magic of love to define your words and move your actions. Go ahead."

"Oh, now I understand why you are still single. It could be your lack of knowledge about building relations," I said rather nastily and impertinently.

It took me a few seconds to realise what I had said. I felt sorry for being so rude but then words cannot be taken back. They must have pierced his heart through and through and suddenly I noticed a tear roll down from his eyes. How could I have been so callous?

"I am sorry, Uncle D," I said. "Please, forgive me. I did not mean to say that."

Uncle D nodded his head knowingly and went to his bedroom, where I noticed he picked up his syringe and began spraying a message. When he ended his task, he turned to me without saying a word. I was really angry at myself for my stupidity.

I drew near him and saw what he had written: 'Deep in my heart, I am concealing things that I have never said, afraid that you will slip away.'

"What? I am unable to grasp the message," I said.

But he stood silent like a wall. There was no reaction from him for quite some time before he gathered the courage to narrate his life story.

"Why did you not tell me anything about yourself so far?" I asked feeling sad and astonished.

"Son, my life story is there but I wanted to wait till the right time to tell you all. Remember there is always a story behind every success and the story may at times be open like a book or it could be kept under wraps."

"Please do tell me what it is as I am longing to hear it from your mouth." I was really surprised because it had never struck me that there could be something or someone in my uncle's life. It then struck me that I had been so engrossed in my own sorrows and pleasures that I had not ever thought of asking him about his life.

Uncle D began, "I had thought that I would hide all about myself from this world but now, seeing you in a situation which seems somewhat like mine, I am tempted to tell you my entire story. Today I feel the time has come to divulge my story and through it make you realise the importance of love over the word 'practical'."

We went and sat down in the conference room where Uncle D began to narrate his life story.

The story begins...

"I was born in a family which was doing extremely well in the export business. The business was growing tremendously at a fast pace, keeping my Dad busy, day and night. Even, my Mom was pre-occupied in supporting Dad by accompanying him to social gatherings which had become quite an integral part of my Dad's life. Being the only child of my parents, I found myself all alone, fending for myself. To overcome my loneliness, I began to look for new friends, new games, anything at all which could hold my attention and keep me happy. My parents, even when they were at home, had no time to spare for me and seemed unconcerned about me. They were more concerned about their balance-sheets, their share prices, their rivals in the market, the glamour, the brands and all that which accompanies such a fast life. My Mom had no time to be bothered about her only son.

"My Dad even did not know in which class I studied. Once my parents insisted on my accompanying them to a party as other children too were invited and there a business colleague asked him where and in which class I studied. My father cooked up some name of the school and gave all the wrong information because he had not ever taken personal interest in my education. Here I was a bloody helpless child, who was present in his Dad's life merely as a trademark. I had become sick of the whole thing. I really was tired of it all. I always ended up looking for new friends, new games, everything that could drag me away from the corporate world.

"One thing I must tell you, your Uncle D was a dashing guy, very smart, handsome with brown hair, very refined and polished. I used to speak very politely to all. I could win over anybody by just talking to him or her for a few minutes. That is why people were attracted towards me very easily. Even my female cousins used to flirt with me and call me the show-stealer of the family. My parents were pleased about all this because this gave them the opportunity to go out in society and display me as their product.

"I was just eight-years old when I met Rhea, who was elder to me by seven years. She was the only daughter of my Dad's business partner (Mr Khurana) and a very goodlooking girl with fair complexion, round face, long hair and brown eyes."

"Do you even know what you are saying?" I asked, interrupting him.

"Allow me to continue... She had studied at an all girls' school called the Mussoorie International Girls School. She was not happy to be back home, because just like me, she was disturbed by her parents' materialistic attitude. Like me, she longed to have a close friend. Moreover this was a new place for her. As was to be expected, we both complimented each other and became close friends. Neither of us had any desire to attend those artificial parties, where everything was superficial. We would invariably prefer to stay back at home (sometimes at her place and sometimes at mine) whenever our parents were busy expanding their social circle. We both loved to spend time with each other. We both were frank and open with each other and did things which we wanted. We would play all sorts of games, both indoor and outdoor and at night time, we would experiment with new recipes in the kitchen. The extent of our relationship could be judged from the fact that I joined swimming classes because she had joined them and it meant getting to spend more time together. Bound to our traditional culture, we were considered brother and sister by society and I addressed her as Rhea Didi."

"That's obvious! You are sounding as if there was something mysterious..." I said, but he continued unmindful of the interruption.

"On one of the casual night stays at her home, we were playing 'Ludo' and she became tired of throwing the dice again and again. She threw the game away and pestered me to think of a new game. We both mulled for the next few minutes before she said, 'Let us discuss our school life.'

"At that time I came to know that she had been in a girls' school all her life and planned to continue with the same. You know how girls from girls' schools are like. They are really desperate for sex. If they cannot find a way to give vent to their sexual urges, they tend to create one and that is what Rhea did. She asked me, 'Which games do you play at school?'

"Like any other normal child, I listed all the indoor and outdoor games that I had learned since the time I was born.

"She continued, 'Is there any special game that you play only with a girl, when you both are alone?'

"'No, I play only scrabble and such games with a girl but I can play them with a boy too,' I replied innocently."

"Wait! Wait! Uncle D, what are you trying to say? It is sounding rather bizarre," I interrupted.

"I know it may seem disgusting but the bloody reality that transpired with your Uncle D was that she insisted on finding out about sex from me. In truth, I knew nothing about the subject and moreover what else could you expect from an eight-year old child?"

"She said, 'Okay, Drishya, we will play a new game today.'

"Like any other normal child, I was persuaded and was damn excited to learn a new game from my Rhea Didi.

"'Before playing the game, learn all the rules of the game,' she told me. 'It's a very special game; it is not like any other game, say Ludo, carom or something. It is very special and it will be between just you and me. First of all, you will not call me Didi while playing the game. The code name for the game is 'Darling' in which we will call each other 'Darling' during the game, but mind you, it is only during the game. It is to be played only when we both are alone, preferably in a closed room, so that the others cannot notice us. You will play this game only with me and promise me that you will not tell anybody about it, otherwise I will never play this game again. Remember, this is the most important rule.'

"After I had given her my promise, I noticed that she began to dress in a raunchy style; it was not her normal appearance. She switched off all the lights, leaving only a lamp lighted and said, 'Are you ready to play?'

"I was perplexed but could not contain my excitement at playing a new game. We both were seated on the bed. She tilted her head sideways and leaned towards me suddenly and kissed me on my lips.

"I was taken aback and moved a bit backward (as I had never done something like that earlier and I felt awkward), asking, 'What are you trying to do?'

"'It's a game. You will learn to enjoy it soon,' she replied plainly. She again kissed my lips with my face held in her hands. She ordered me to suck in and I did as told. I soon began to enjoy it all. Next, she ordered me to open my mouth and I did that. Then my tongue was on hers and hers on mine and we were engaged in the French kiss, like wild animals. We were smooching with each other. She kissed my face, my lips, my neck, my tongue and I did the same to her. Yes, I began to enjoy it all.

"She slipped her T-shirt off her shoulder and told me to kiss and I did. I was enticed by the pleasure, the fragrance of her body, the warmth that I had never experienced before. I turned from one shoulder to another, from front to her back, kissing and kissing like a wild animal and enjoying it all. She dragged my hand inside her T-shirt, which was a crazy feeling as I moved my hand over her naked body, sliding from her waist to her complete back. Sometimes she would constrict and expand, producing strange voices, and sometimes embrace me hard while kissing wildly. We both lay down in her bed and did the same. Soon she was over me and then we rolled and I was over her. It was no less than heaven, lying above a naked girl with such seductive movements. I was then moving my hands over the softest curves of a female body – her bosom. She pulled her T-shirt up to her breast and allowed me to do the cunnilingus activities. Finally, she took off her T-shirt and then her bra. I kissed her cuddly soft breasts, pressed them, kissed her whole naked body right from her neck to her waist, where sliding my hand to the border of her panty. I moved my hand on her naked back, moving up and down as she panted wildly. I felt as if I had conquered the world.

"I hadn't attained puberty but my sex organs were responding. I just wanted to do it once more, though I did not know how to manage it all. I was unaware of what was happening. She was in her teens and had attained puberty. So she used my hand for fingering. Obviously, my dick was of no use for her at that time as it could not perform miracles at that age," he said, laughing.

"Did you enjoy it all?" I asked.

"Yep! Boys are allured by each and every sex organ of a girl and I was encountering them all at once. Though I could not do anything much then, but the pleasure was there in such adventures."

He continued, "After all the cunnilingus activities, the game was over with both the players fatigued out. Subsequently, whenever we got the opportunity, we both played this unnamed game. It would not be wrong on my part to say that I had been trapped into the sexual activity, but it was not at my instigation. It was the pleasure I got from it – the feeling of kissing someone so wildly, sliding your hand on a girl's naked body, pressing her soft boobs with your hands, lying down over a nude girl – it is all inexplicable and inevitably great.

"That was how I passed my childhood, involved in sexual activities, despite being a stranger to the word 'sex', with a plucky girl, who believed in excelling by hook or by crook. She used me for her own sexual pleasure, playing a scam in the name of a game.

"As time passed, she cleared her Class XII and left home to pursue higher studies. It was damn easy for a girl like her to indulge with other guys as she was really desperate for sex. To play with a child no longer held any attraction for her and so she moved on. But what happened was that I could no longer refrain myself from playing that game as I really enjoyed it. It gave me the pleasure that no other thing could. It was more than life for me and I could not get over those contretemps encounter. I just wanted to continue playing that game.

"But neither did I get the opportunity nor was Rhea ready to play the game again. So, I was left as the bloody helpless child. Once I thought about revealing my problem to my parents, but I was bound to the rules of the game. I wanted to play the game at any cost, but Rhea had gone far from me. I was left alone.

"With the passing of time and growing age, I realised the indigestible fact of being misused by Rhea. She had used me for her sexual pleasure."

I smirked. Uncle D noticed and looked at me suspiciously. To divert his attention from my smile, I asked, "So, you told all this to your parents after realising the fact that you had been 'misused'?"

I was never a bad boy...

Uncle D replied, "I thought over it but never did reveal it because it could have damaged the relationship between my Dad and his business partner. Also I did not want to earn my parents' sympathies for what I had gone through. But I held them responsible for what I had been exposed to as such a tender age. Had they taken proper care of me, no outsider could have had the guts to even touch me but the fact was that a girl had seduced me. I had nobody to turn to or discuss or share my problem, my situation and everything. I hated them for all this. They could not look after me properly, and when they had no time for me, why the hell did they give birth to me? I hated them; I developed a strong grudge against them.

"I began to feel that my entry into this world was merely accidental due to the carelessness of my parents who were busy deriving sexual pleasure out of each other. This gap widened between my parents and me as years passed and I became a misanthrope. They didn't have time to give me attention and did not even care whether I dressed in blue or black. They invariably needed me at social get-togethers so that they could display their product to the society; the beautiful showcase that some did not have, to make them feel jealous. I hated those parties because they were the most important thing for my parents. Gradually I discovered that I began to love those parties because at least for that period of time, I had my parents with me.

"There came a time when I held my first glass of whisky in my hand and I had heard that it could heal all the sorrows in the heart and forget reality. It took me no time to become prey to the habit of drinking. Alcohol began to flow through my food-pipe; its bitter taste searing through my stomach and making me crave for more. Every time I drank, I kept losing myself and realising the reality of life. I began to consider myself a loser and started drinking simply to forget the fact that I had been misused in life. I felt like a burden on earth, a guy of no use to society, a guy who had been misused by others simply because his parents had no time for him.

"I started to smoke and take drugs, thinking that all my sorrows would fly away in the air. But the more I smoked, the more my sorrows increased. As the smoke filled my lungs, I could feel my brain losing the ability to think. It became a way to escape from reality where I could forget all that I had experienced in life. But by the time the feeling of levitation ended and my brain began to take over control, I began to hallucinate and imagine fighting a battle with myself. I began to smoke day and night. I would bunk my school to smoke and soon became a chain-smoker.

"But all my efforts proved fruitless; each time the magic of the drugs ended, I was back to the reality, pushing myself hard to run away from myself. As a result, I screwed my entire education, getting through by scoring just the passing marks which I could manage after being present in the classes, for which my parents paid.

"I was initiated into drugs so that I could escape from reality, but the power of drugs was so intense that I would create a new world, an illusionary world in which I would use prostitutes in order to take my revenge against Rhea. I found that slowly drugs became my most urgent need, my life, without which I could not survive. Life became a myth and drugs ruled my senses, my breath, my thoughts and me. Whenever, I didn't get them, I would look for alternatives so as to escape from the real world. I would spray a deodorant on the socks that I wore as it gave me immense pleasure and after ten days, I would soak the socks in water and drink that water. I know it sounds ridiculous but I did all that. I tried out smack too and that led to increased expenses. My parents were not bothered about the expenses and I cannot deny that if nothing else, they provided me money.

"My problems increased because I would have difficulty in not being able to sleep because I saw her in my dreams playing that same game, asking me to kiss. I still wonder why they were all bad dreams! In this period, I developed the philosophy that I wanted to play that game with any girl whatsoever. Now

I had a dick that could satisfy all their needs. I developed a superiority complex and my Dad's tremendous bank-balance offered me the means to impress any girl. My personality, my oratory skills and my name began to draw girls towards me like bees to honey and every other stupid girl was now a victim of this raunchy guy. I would take drugs before every sexual escapade and imagine making love to Rhea. I could not fathom why I was doing all this and what was happening to me.

"After getting lost in the world of drugs, I would get pleasure from kissing the whole body of my victim. Each encounter made me see an image of Rhea in her. I just wanted to prove to her that I had not flunked. I did have the dick to perform miracles and my love-making became acts of aggression on my victims. I loved doing it all, while the silly girls would lap it up all. They were so dumb that they were willing to become my slaves and I was the lucky one to satisfy all their requirements and even destroy the virginity of some of them.

"I met them in clubs, pubs, wherever possible and though I knew I was ruining my life, yet I wanted to retaliate against Rhea. I even stepped into brothels when I did not find a girl any other way. I was ready to pay for the game. Those girls were not much different, except for the fact that they charged money for their services. In each and every girl that I slept with, I saw a reflection of Rhea and that pushed me to give her the best shot of my life ever. The reality was that I had not forgotten Rhea."

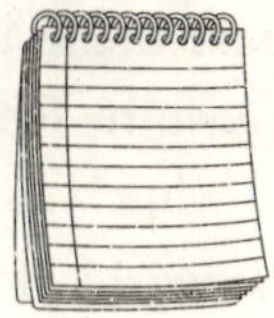

Life took a turn like a coin.........

I could not believe all what Uncle D told me because to me he seemed like an extinct volcano. Now it seemed he had been lying dormant, ready to erupt at the right moment. How could a person who had been through so much, seen so much, become so calm and cool today as if he was an angel of peace and not the owner of the Angel Empire? Suddenly I asked him, "Who is Angel?"

"Don't you know this, Aditya?" he almost yelled and continued, "It was my mother's name..."

"Wait! Wait! Here angel is used for a male, *nah*!" I interrupted.

"Hey boy, you're quite intelligent. When I was a child, she told me that angels are messengers of God from heaven and come to help you out on earth. Now for a five-year old child, Mom seemed a virtual angel to me and since that day I began to call her Angel. An innocent child could not differentiate between a male and a female," he clarified.

"Crap! I thought it would be linked to one of your female friends."

"Yeah, you can say that or maybe you cannot."

"What do you mean by that?" I queried.

"I will tell you, dude. I am here to open the pages for you to read them, son," he winked and continued to open the pages of his life story.

"I became a true Casanova. I destroyed many lives, slept with a number of girls, whose names I don't even remember, but I do recall that they all were great. They all seemed amazingly good in bed. Actually every naked girl looked good and I was the king in bed. I loved them all but life does turn like a coin.

"After acquiring my graduation degree, as usual, I was out on my sexual sprees, when a girl entered my life. I had completely given up but then it happened to me – the sweetest thing that could ever be. She was like a fantasy, a dream. The first day I saw her, time stood still. Here was one for whom I had taken birth as a man. I had not seen such gentleness in any person ever before. She was so pristine, so calm and composed. She was just an ordinary looking girl but there was something special about her that performed the miracle to keep me bound to her.

"Scientists say that if a man gazes at a girl for more than 8.2 seconds, he likes her but I kept on looking at her for more than 30 minutes and that time interval was enough to make me fall in love with her. I kept looking at her, discovering her every moment – her charming dimples, her childish attitude, her way of rotating her eyeballs in a circle, her smile, her hair curling down her cheeks before settling down behind her ears. I was held spellbound and she performed the magic while sitting at one corner table. For the first time in my life I could not think of anything else except for meeting her. She directly entered my heart from my eyes. I realised there and then that she was the one for me, the one who would change my life, the one whom I could marry. She was an ordinary-looking girl but she had cast an extraordinary spell over me. The magic of love, the magic that was far above all the pleasures that all kinds of drugs and girls had given, was nothing in front of her serenity. There was something wonderful and beautiful about her that could change the world around me in few seconds. I began to visualise a new world with her. I fell in love with her that day and came to realise the meaning of love.

"When I closed my eyes to check whether it was all real, I realised her face had the ability to cast a special effect, as it made me see heaven all around me for the first time in my life. I knew she was the one for me and I would marry her. Suddenly, I found the boy sitting next to her in front of me, address me gently and offer his hand for a handshake, before saying, 'Hello!'

"I stammered and shook hands, 'Hello!'

"Oh God, I couldn't desist from looking at her directly and a hoarse voice at my side remarked, 'Remember, we met on your Dad's party?'

'Yeah, last weekend,' I made a wild guess.

'Your Dad is a great person. He...' he continued talking while I continued looking at her.

'Sorry, I didn't remember your name?' I interrupted him, becoming tired of hearing so much about my Dad.

'It's Shubh, sir!' he replied generously.

'Stop calling me, sir. The name is Drishya,' I said laughingly.

'I know it,' he shot back.

'Then, use it. Okay Shubh?'

'Yes, Drishya.'

'Hey! Who is the girl with you? I guess, she was not there at the party that day?' (I knew she was not, else I would have seen her.)

'No, she's my cousin Angel.' (Gosh, the same name I had been using since I was a five-year old was the name of this girl, who had captured my imagination.)

'What?' I squealed

'Sorry! The name is Angellica. We call her Angel. She has just completed her graduation and is now here to enjoy.'

'Can I?' I asked politely, pointing towards her.

'Sure!'

"Shubh introduced me to Angel (I noticed that she was dressed in a completely white dress, like a gown) and I was shocked to find myself, an experienced person, stammering in front of her. All I could manage to say was to tell her that my name was Drishya, the one who had lost all his vision watching her. I managed to note down Shubh's number to keep in touch with them. I could not sleep that night, as I kept on thinking of her. The pleasure of seeing her face all around my eyes kept me awake the whole night. I had fallen in love. I began to smile for no reason except for remembering her smile. My heart, my brain, all had fallen prey to her. I was in love and I wanted to announce this to anybody at all who would have cared to listen.

"When I learned that Shubh was her brother and she had come out with him, it meant that they were used to going out together. I tried to keep a tab on their movements and followed them from place to place in order to draw closer to them. I found that every time that I saw her, my love for her increased by leaps and bounds. I had really become crazy and I wanted to marry her. Life had changed; everything seemed beautiful. I gave up smoking, drinking, drugs and all. My days and nights passed in just thinking about the moments spent with her and planning the next opportunity to catch up with her. I had undergone a complete metamorphosis.

"Soon, Shubh became aware of the feelings I harboured for his cousin and anyway it was all very apparent from the way I talked to her, the way I would keep looking at her that even a blind man could see my love for her. Shubh told me, "She likes you, too." (Those words gave a new life to me.)

"From what I was, I had changed for the better and I knew it. I had started respecting others and no more harboured the desire to take revenge. I held no grudges against anybody. I wanted to forget my past, just make love to her, gaze at her, talk to her and spend time with her.

"One day, Shubh took me to his place for lunch. I enjoyed looking at Angel, busy as she was cooking and serving the food. She very rarely threw her cute smile at me. Her Mom seemed like a psychic case and was very possessive about her daughter (it was understandable if you had such a cute daughter). She was very close to her Mom and I liked it too.

"Two hearts began to beat as one but I wondered whether it was love for her or not! How could a guy like me love someone? To check out on myself, I invited a girl named Radhika for a date and took her to bed. We both lay semi-naked near each other, but I found that I had no desire to take her. None of my organs responded to her touch. She held my hand in hers and dragged it on her naked body, right from back to the front, asking me to do something wild, but there was no response from me. While lying with her, my thoughts were centred on Angel. Her cute face filled my mind and finally, Radhika said, "Who is the lucky girl, you bastard, who has captured your imagination?" I knew the answer and I wanted to tell her that she was not the one! She had made me realise that I was in love.

"I wanted to talk to Shubh and then thought of telling his cousin directly that I wanted to marry her but only after revealing everything about my past. At the same time I was frightened that she might refuse to have anything to do with me after hearing about my past. Anyway I wanted an honest start to a new relationship, a most respectful relationship in my life.

I began to consider myself a real bastard for having played with the lives of so many girls simply to take revenge against one who had messed up my life. How could I be so callous as to use them and then discard them as if they were dirt? Any one of them could have easily spoiled my life by just complaining about me, but none did that. They had all loved me and cared about my well-being. How great the girls had been with me and it was too late to realise it.

"If life had taken me on the wrong path, why did I allow my life to flow with the wind? I knew I was being wrong yet I continued with my wrongdoings as if overpowered by the sexual urge. The fact was that I was a bloody loser. I had started hating myself because I had my own reasons for that.

"I love the world,
and the world loves me.
Even then I don't know,
why I hate myself?
I loved myself, when I was free,
but hate myself now when I have grown into a tree.
The chains have bound me,
carried me away,
Now I realise,
I am far behind from where I have to stay.
I acquired success,
but not of mine.
It maybe a wonder for others,
but for me it was happiness for a moment of time.
My dreams were influenced by the greed of others,
my life had become a stretcher dragged by others.
Now I felt shy in front of Him.
I wanted to cry in front of Him,
He who had created me to reach the sky,

but I was sorry I could not even jump high enough to reach that high.

The world loves me
and I love the world.
Even then, I do not know why I hate myself?

"That was the first and the last poem ever written by Drishya Roy but I loved it Aditya because I had penned it out of my true feelings and it was all a true fact."

"So, how did you propose to her?" I asked (he was lost somewhere.)

He continued, "It took me three months to gather the strength to confess the sins I had committed. Finally, one fine day, I took her out on an evening walk to an old temple after taking permission from Shubh. I trembled with fear all the way because I was afraid that I would lose her. But I had to confess my sins to her. I was determined to let her know the truth of the person she would have to think of marrying. We sat down on the steps leading to the temple, I kept my hand over her hand in her lap and blurted all that I had done in life. Not once did I dare to look up at her face, frightened as I was of being rebuked by her. I told her all about Rhea, alcohol, drugs, brothels, Radhika and finally how had I changed after meeting her."

"What did she say?" I asked excitedly.

"Guess?" he winked at me with an irritating smile on his face (he could be so childish at times).

"Obviously, no," I replied instantly.

"No, Aditya, girls are really great. They can understand the pain and the sufferings of others."

"You mean she said 'yes'?" I asked.

"Yes!" he said with a smile on his face.

"How could she?" I wondered.

"Promise me, you won't interrupt me next time," he said and continued, "She was amused and said, 'Thank God I have found an experienced guy, as I'm too bad with all this'."

"What? She was actually smiling and saying all this?" I asked.

He replied, "I don't know. I did not dare to look up at her. I noticed a tear fall on my hand and it was then that I looked at her face. Her eyes had become moist with tears and her eyes revealed sympathy for me. She looked ravishingly pretty with her face covered with tears. She had realised that the fault was not entirely mine but circumstances had played a joke and disturbed the tenor of my life so ruthlessly that I had got lost. I had become a poor victim of the circumstances.

"She leaned forward for a kiss but I pulled myself away as I hated myself. I could not believe how I could manage to win over such a pure and pristine girl? I couldn't believe it all.

"I asked her to think over it all before coming to any decision and added, 'Are you sure you will be able to live with a guy who has spoiled the lives of so many innocent girls like you?'

"I want to be with you Drishya throughout my life. I love you," she said simply.

"I was simply baffled to hear those words and I felt she was even better than what I had expected. I could not believe my luck and kept on asking myself, 'Is this real or a fantasy?' because it was no less than any fairytale.

'Do think over it all. Just analyse me once,' I stammered.

"'I have never analysed you and neither do I want to. I just love you for whatever you are and I want to be with you for the rest of my life. Whatever you are for the world, it does not matter; what matters is what you are for me. You are my love; one whom I love limitlessly, who is special to me, who is different from this world and with whom I feel complete.' She said it all so charmingly that it brought tears to my eyes. I would have kissed her but I don't know from where a thought came to my mind, 'Would I ever be able to do it with one who is so pure?'

"She insisted that she was ready for me but I could not take her on it! I left the place and asked her to think over it again before coming to any decision. I was willing to wait for her answer as long as she wished. On leaving the place, I began to cry, sobbing uncontrollably because I knew that we loved each other, complimented each other and accepted our love. But how was it possible for her to spend the rest of her life with a bastard like me, who had taken to bed so many girls?

"What troubled me also was the fact that probably she was drawn to me out of sympathy for me. I simply did not want her to love me out of sympathy or pity. Maybe, I had misunderstood the situation because in love, it is never sympathy but care and consideration that count. I could not fathom why she loved me despite my shortcomings, which were one too many. I knew that females of the human species were emotionally and mentally much more stronger than their male counterparts, but one silly mistake committed out of sentimentality could make them regret their action forever.

"She told me that she had spoken to her Mom and revealed to her the desire to marry me. She was very close to her Mom who was like her best friend. No mother could have allowed her daughter to marry a guy who had spoiled the lives of so many girls in the past. Many days passed after my meeting with her but no reply came. I presumed that it had all come to an end as her mother could not have agreed to her daughter's choice. She must have thought over it practically and decided to refuse. I was worried but did not have the strength to approach her.

"One day I learned that she had got married to someone else. My Angel had gone. Later, after her wedding I was informed by Shubh that she still loved me but under her mother's pressure, she had relented to marry a stranger.

"I had been a victim of time. Life had played such a cruel joke on me that I could not even stand and face the world: But was it entirely my fault?

"My life again took a turn for the worse. I became reckless and started to burn my Dad's money, dancing to the beats of music in an inebriated state brought on by alcohol and drugs. I was back to my aimless life but no more interested in sex. I began to lose myself, wanting to meet my end. I even tried to commit suicide but that required guts which a loser like me couldn't muster.

"But do you know what? Things happen when they have to. While roaming on the roads, one day my eyes fell on a poster which read as follows: 'Why parents are next to God?' Do you really want to know why it caught my attention? It is human nature to be allured towards things that you hate or have all the reasons to prove them wrong. I noted down the venue and the timing because I had always thought that parents become parents accidentally in between the game of sexual pleasure. They do not have the time to look after their dependants, so why are they considered next to God? The society has always kept parents busy as they, while developing their social circle, forget that they have children waiting for them at home. As a result of their ignorance, here was a bloody loser with nothing to do in life. I was only certainly breathing in air and breathing it out, though I could not tell why I was alive in the world. I should have been cremated or buried in a grave. I was certain that I would stop breathing the moment I started to concentrate on myself.

"Coming back to the poster I had seen, I went to attend the lecture merely to check out the extent of the grudge I had against my parents. What was so special that other parents did and what my parents had not ever thought of doing?

"I found myself seated among all the aged people when I attended the lecture. I noticed a majority of them were above the age of fifty except for a few, who were in their late thirties. Some old couples too were present, possibly to check out what the speaker had to say or possibly they had nothing better to do.

"I just hated my parents. They had never taken care of me; they had left me with Rhea, who used me, and they did not try to reform me despite knowing I was landing in all kinds of situations that were liable to screw my life. Even today, I do not have them by my side.

"The stage at the venue of the lecture had a wooden stand in one corner and a big banner with a photograph of the speaker in the centre His name was inscribed at the top as Dineshji. When he stood up to speak, I noticed a man in his late forties take up the mike to speak. He might have retired from a professional job to do what he liked more, I suppose."

That really changed my life...

He began again, “A winning horse does not know why he runs in the race. He runs out of pain and misery on being flogged. For us humans, life is a race and God is the rider who is constantly putting all kinds of obstacles in order to check out our diligence and desire to succeed because He really wants us to win and yes, run on our own legs.”

“That is how he began his lecture and I liked it when he said that in every difficulty lies an opportunity.

“He continued, ‘How many of us really believe it to be true? Actually no one because, as human beings, we get lost in our problems and do not have the time to think of the opportunities lying ahead and take them up. However, there are a few great human beings among us all over this universe and who are ardent followers of these great words and try to follow them in life. Can you guess who they are?

'What is the first word a child speaks when he's born? Yes, it is Ma, mother. Can you guess how much pain a mother has to bear when a baby is born? No one can. Even the lady in front of me cannot remember the pain she must have borne though she must be a mother because the moment of pain has been forgotten to be replaced with the pleasure of holding an infant in her arms and that gives her the strength to bear the pain of nurturing her young one. Actually, that is the greatest pain to exist in this world. Scientifically, it is greater than the pain experienced on the breakage of 42 bones in the body at the same time. It leads to rupturing of the skin to permit the delivery of a mass of skin and tender bones out of the body, where it has developed since the last nine months. The mother feeds the infant her own milk to help it develop into a human being after undergoing severe pain at not only delivering the child but also to make the little one see the world. That is the spirit of every mother. She willingly bears all the pain just to hear her infant's first cry. That is what is actually called the birthday – the day when a mother smiles watching her child wail and it is her grit and determination that help her withstand all the pain. She keeps pushing herself to sail through tough times and find the real happiness. This is because she knows that within every difficulty lies an opportunity.

'The mother has the capability to see that the one who will get to see the beautiful world will one day become her helping hand. The pain of nine months will offer her a lifetime of happiness. That is why she is considered *janani*, the one to give birth. Is it any wonder that in the older times, a woman was worshipped as a goddess? It is her farsightedness that makes her special, different from a normal human being, different from the rest of the world. This is the reason why she is so important for the one who is starting a new life.

'She knows that this bundle of joy will bring her great happiness during troublesome times.'

"He then concluded with the poem:

'Parents and parents,
they inspire your talents.
They are the living gods on earth,
they are the most loving creatures on earth.
They burn themselves to give light to you,
they bend themselves to give flight to you.
They are always concerned about your care,
they are always with you through unfair and fair.
They do hard work to turn your dreams into reality,
although that means their own dreams would shatter.
They take in their stride every pity,
so that you must not face any difficulty.
They accept you as their soul,
you become their lifetime goal.
They do every possible thing to make you pure,
it is because of them that you are called the most wanted 'allure'.
But you isolate them, when they need you to survive,
leaving them behind without caring about their life.
Remember that you're a part of them,
you've been nurtured with great care by them.

Remember, the day they held your hand during the first walk,
remember, they made you able to talk.
Serve them and seek their blessings,
otherwise, you'll get from Him strong dressings.
But I see children having grudges against their parents,
parents who feel proud at their child's success
when the child can't bear a word from his parents' mouth.
I just need to remind you to remember those who have taught you A to Z.
Just think if they had grudged your kick on their face when you were a child,
they would have killed you for your act.
Just remember, how much of their time you wasted when you shit in your clothes irresponsibly,
just think and talk to yourself and realise.
If you kiss their feet the whole of your life
you would still not be able to repay their debts
So please serve them happily.
If you do not have any other reason to live
then learn to live for them.

'We usually say that love is not a thing to show. If you love your parents or anyone from the bottom of your heart, then show it to them. Just think of a mother who kisses her child endlessly, hugs him all the time. She is not doing it to show off to the world. She is simply in love and is making the others realise that he is important. Therefore, is it any wonder that when the child is born, he cries out her name?'

"Everyone clapped and so I did. The one thing really great about that lecture was that time was given to the audience to ponder upon the reality. The realisation really changed my life and offered a new vision to me.

"When the lights were switched on, I could see many parents had tears rolling down their cheeks. And do you know that a tear rolled down my cheek too? That day I understood the reason why it was my duty to breathe in air and breathe out, why I should eat and drink, why I should survive and live. It was all for my parents if not for myself. I was once again left feeling ashamed at blaming them for everything. They were the ones who made things and life possible for me. I again began to feel guilty for not having spent time with them, lost as I was in the bloody game of taking revenge against Rhea. As a result all I had done was to increase the schism between us. I should have tried to understand their situation too, for come to think of it, all that they were doing was to provide for my happiness and well-being, so that I would not have to slog in life when I grew up. They were undoubtedly great, but I had failed to recognise their worth. I decided then to spend the rest of my life with my parents for they were my life.

"I kept thinking and remembering the happy times I had spent with them in the long past. I returned home at 2:00 a.m. with the firm determination to devote myself completely to them. I found them asleep when I went to their room. I was really desperate to talk to them, to tell them how selfish and self-centred I had been. I had to show some conciliatory action towards them and after pondering for some time, sat down to write a letter to them.

> "Dear Mom and Dad,
>
> I am sorry for the things I have done and the things that I might do in future, but one thing for sure that I really want to do

is to spend the rest of my life with you. I had grudges against you both but I never brought them to your notice. I know I had crossed the limits of bad behaviour which I did not realise then, but which I find was simply uncalled for on my part. It is now I realise that it was not your fault at all. It was my fault for turning out to be what I did. I slipped at every step in my life, despite knowing that I was being wrong but once caught in the morass, I did not know how to stop or get out of it. I kept on falling into quicksand because the devil had taken possession of me, but now I want to change. I just want to live as your son, a normal human being.

I ignored you, holding you responsible for turning out the way I did and did not even talk to you properly out of anger and frustration. But now I realise how foolish I had been to act so immaturely. I have got my life because of you but I spoilt it, causing you misery and myself suffering and pain. My body was purely a gift from you and my soul has been nurtured by you. If today I am praised for my gift of the gab, it is entirely inherited from you Dad and you rule my mind. Above all, my name Drishya is also a blessing from you. The greatest thing that I realise now is that you never asked me for anything in response. You did it all so selflessly, just to see a smile on my face. You never thought of yourself in front of my happiness, but because of me the gap widened between us. I know that if you were to bend your head in front of God, you would always ask for my happiness without caring for your needs. You did it all just for me and that is why I believe that I am the luckiest child born to be provided so much of everything and all kinds of comforts. And what did I give you in return? Nothing, just nothing at all. You trusted me blindly and that really makes me feel special today.

I have always lived life on my own terms, believing in doing things, without thinking of how it might hurt you or harm your reputation. I never cared about you, but I am no more that irresponsible Drishya. Now I care for you and I am going to live only for you. I want to spend the rest of my life with you and die for you.

Your loving son,
Drishya

"I left the letter on my Dad's study table and went to sleep. The next morning when I woke up, my parents had left for another world. They both died in an accident. They had left the house for a business meeting in the early morning hours to catch their flight and met with an accident. I had been expecting them to stay back after reading the letter, but for all you know, maybe they did not get to even see it. Their car was struck by a loaded truck coming from the opposite direction and they were killed on the spot. I just could not come to terms with their death. It was so shocking that only a day earlier I had realised their importance in my life and how much I loved them but the next day they had left this world, leaving a void in my life. It was all a cruel joke played by Fate. I did not even get the chance to hug them properly. I did not even get to know whether they had read my letter or not. I attended to all the rites and rituals to be performed, but what was the use of it all now? Both my gods had left me all alone and sorry for my behaviour. Was the cost of my sins so high that it had to be settled through the death of my parents?

"The most traumatising day of my life passed, with me losing all interest in everything around me. I went to their room to feel their presence around me and I found the letter at the same place where I had kept it. But I just picked it up to take it away when my eyes fell on the line written below my last sentence. They had written,

'We too love you, Drishya.

Your loving Mom and Dad.'"

Uncle D showed me the letter that he always kept in his pocket as that had been the one and only conversation between him and his parents. I could see a tear roll down his cheek as he opened the letter to show it to me. In the next second, I saw him sob uncontrollably as if he wanted to wash away all his sins and wrongs through his tears. I had never seen him cry before. He was sobbing like a three-year old child.

I tried to console him, "Uncle D, whatever has happened was destined to happen. Human beings have no control over fate as we are like puppets in our Creator's hands. Try to control yourself because crying will not bring your parents back on earth."

"Yeah, I know it all, buddy. I am not crying. I know it all. Life has to move on and continue. I know it all, son." he said, wiping away his tears with the sleeves of his shirt.

"So, what's next?" I said, trying to change the topic.

"What?" he mumbled hoarsely.

"Angel Empire!"

"Oh, you really want to know about it, my son?" He got up and picked up his Dad's personal diary.

He said, "Dad was in the habit of maintaining a diary because he believed it helped to relate you to your loved ones, especially when you are unable to express your feelings to them. I picked the diary up and I really could feel him around me – his calm voice calling out my name, his soft hands patting me on my head, consoling me when things went wrong and saying, 'I am there for you son. Why do you worry son? I love you.' I had wanted to tell him the same thing but it was too late now because he was no longer alive. I tired to seek his forgiveness in my mind and I do it again and again even today, but what is the use? He has gone far, far away from me, from my follies. I wish I could see my parents at least once so that I could hug them and tell them how much I love them. I want someone to share my feelings but who can realise how difficult it is to survive after losing your loved ones? When I read his diary from page to page, I was shocked to discover that he had even jotted down what I was wearing on a particular day. I remember him telling my Mom, 'Today Drishya is looking great and do you know why? This is because he is my son, the son of a successful businessman. The other day the orange outfit that he had worn did not suit him. Do not make him wear the same colour again. He looks best in black, which is the colour of royalty. He actually is royal because everything of mine is for him only.' Now I feel how he must have observed me daily though I was not aware of it ever. He never said a word, probably because he thought I would not appreciate it. It is now that I realise how he must have loved me.

"Drowning and drowning in those pages, I got lost in my Dad. I decided to live my life like him only if he were to come back to earth. I wanted to plead with him, 'Dad, please come back to me and teach me how to live like you.' I was at a stage when I had no control over my tears. On reading further, I discovered that his business had suffered heavy losses for two years but he did never let me know of it. He had ended his diary with the belief that his son would make it flourish one day. The day when he died, they were about to sign an important deal but that was not to be.

"I have now got the reason to live, to walk, to talk, to open my eyes and look around, to breathe in and out and be myself."

"So, that's how the great Angel Empire emerged?" I asked.

"No, that was just like igniting the fire. I am not a magician, who could just wave his hand and get the business running. I realised that I was nothing but then I saw the potential of being a zero and I simply began to work upwards from it."

"Please explain this in detail, so that I too could learn a lesson from it."

"Oh, *bachcha* has grown up and wants to learn new things in life. Well, let me tell you it is nothing but a way to live life. When you are at level zero, you want to learn the maximum from life. So first of all, accept yourself to be there, especially if you are stranger to it all and a new face to the business world. It is like knocking on the door of life to derive the maximum knowledge in your life. That's what I feel personally because it is then that you become interested enough to grasp the nitty-gritty of life and apply it to your work. To be able to do every possible thing with this knowledge, you have to be excited enough to learn as a three-year old child."

"I don't get the point."

"I always knew you are a dumbo, Aditya. Allow me to explain it with all the doors of your brain opened."

I bent my head a bit and said, "I am all yours, sir."

He smiled at me and said, "You are so *besharam*," and began again, "today you take only a second to say what you have learnt in your whole life and do not take even a second to think."

"I guess ABC is the only way to answer."

"Here, you have got my point. Before you learnt ABC and all, you knew nothing and therefore you grasped it so well and applied it in every sphere of life. Regular practice of it has implanted the alphabets so deeply that you can never forget them. But as time passes and we grow up into adults, we think that we know everything in the world. We do not want to learn ABC because we do not want to get lost in this sea of knowledge. But one who dives deep into the sea of knowledge is able to discover the pearls of knowledge."

"How did you manage to acquire all this knowledge about the corporate world?" I asked Uncle D.

"To get into the world, you must try to acquire practical knowledge of every aspect of the business you want to try your hand on. So I started with Khurana uncle, who was my Dad's business partner."

"Rhea's Dad!" I screamed with excitement.

"You have said it. I never knew that Rhea was his daughter. Thank you, my boy (he always made fun of me at such times). You must remember that you have to make compromises with a few things in life. I had realised the meaning of my name Drishya was 'the vision to see', the impossible to happen. So it is my vision that had planned this empire. If I wanted to make it really big, right from my heart, I was intelligent enough not to let minor issues overpower me or dominate over me, especially my past."

"But you had to face Rhea!" I said, with both my hands open.

"So that was not a big deal; the big deal was the Angel Empire. I know Rhea's face reminded me of my past history but that did not mean I should sit at one place and cry over my past history. The time had come for me to get up and look towards a bright future. You know one good thing about time is that it makes you act. It only requires that you needs to adjust to new situations. I began my business with my uncle and pursued my studies for completing my MBA side by side. My creative mind paved the path for success and I came up with the concept 'Youngistaan ki democrazy.'"

"I did not know that it was you who actually came out with that concept. I cannot believe what you are saying."

"Obviously, it was purely my idea. Why do you have doubts regarding that?"

I wondered how a single human being could do it all. I was perturbed about it and seeing my face, he said, "You are looking peeved, is it not? You are not able to believe it all."

"Yup!"

"First of all you go and cook 'Maggi' as I am dying to eat it. Put in your best effort to make 'Maggi' really taste special as you must have started respecting me by this time."

We both went to the kitchen and I quietly worked on preparing the 'Maggi' so that it would turn out to be the best that he could have eaten so far. I was silently attending to my chore, not because I had nothing to talk about, but out of respect for him as it had risen tremendously within a short period of time.

I was thinking of Angelica all the while. If he loved her so much, he must be feeling her presence around him also at times. I wanted to meet that incredible beauty who could steal Uncle's heart and still occupy his thoughts.

"Have you ever met Angel after that?" I could not refrain myself from asking.

"Yes, I see her in my dreams daily. She crops up at the most unusual of moments, especially when I am asleep. I am happy that I get to look at her in my dreams at least," he said, smilingly.

"I am serious! Have you ever come face to face with her?"

He tried to avoid answering but seeing my persistence, he had no alternative but to speak out the truth. While I concentrated on the 'Maggi', which I had put on the gas stove and the water had begun to boil, he began, "Yes, there are two reasons behind this Angel Empire. One is that I wanted to pay a tribute to my parents, who were responsible for bringing me on this planet and the other is that I always wanted to prove to Angel's mother that she was wrong. I wanted to prove to her the power of my love – how passionately I loved her daughter that I named my business after her and I will continue to love her till my last breath. I do not want to get her; I just want to love her. That is why when our company entered the telecom department, I invited her Mom as the chief guest."

"Gosh, then it was Mrs Anju Chawla?"

"Yeah, she is that lady. My Angel accompanied her. Mrs Chawla must have realised her mistake and was present on the occasion with her daughter Angel. You know Aditya, there is only guilt in my life. Why? Why did I stop when Angel was ready for her first kiss? Why did I not allow both of us to get together? Why did I not exercise my will over her when she was ready for it all? Why did I allow her to leave me so easily? Why did I give in so easily, without putting up a fight? Was I such a big coward as to allow my love to go away from me in spite of knowing that we both loved each other with our hearts? Why did I behave the way I did? I allowed such a golden opportunity to slip away and the mistake was entirely mine, but the sufferers were two of us."

"Two? You mean Angel and you?" I asked.

"Yep!"

"Why is she suffering?"

"Do you know Aditya, the universal language, the language of love is such that I could not bring myself to go in front of her and greet her. I stayed behind the stage in the camera room, just looking at her. She was the very same Angel, with the same serenity, calmness, elegance, alluring personality. The more I gazed at her, the more my pain increased because I could see grief written large on her face. I could see that she was not happy in her married life and neither am I today as I do not have anyone to look after me. I have been the greatest sinner and have done a grievous harm to such a nice girl (adorable, caring and understanding), who deserved much more than infinite happiness. She did not get anything in life which had been very unfair to her. Had she been with me, definitely she would have been much happier. I thought only about my past which came in the way of my pursuing her. Honestly I did not have the guts to face her parents because I have always tended to run away from reality and that is why I have always been a loser.

"Aditya, I tell you, whatever has happened with you in the past, try to forget it. Think of your present and work for your future. That is why I am asking you to go to Aprajita and talk to her. Keep the doors of your brain closed. Do not think practically but allow your heart to do what it really wants. Let your emotions fly out and let the world know that you are in love. Do not think about the word 'practical' because it can ruin your life. Moreover, she is cent per cent right to say that the most important thing in life is to move on and that is what I did. My problem was that I was not willing to share my love with anyone. I, however, did one thing and that was to keep moving. I am glad she knows the value of it all.

"I have created the Angel Empire which is providing employment and the value of life to so many people but I cannot forget that I committed many mistakes. But that is no big deal. Imperfection defines human beings; we all are full of mistakes, so just keep moving for that is the reason for living. I have kept on moving. Rhea used me, I spoiled many lives, Angel left me, my parents died, but I kept on moving. I promise, you too will find the reason for your life and that day you will experience a great feeling which cannot be described in words. All of us are here on earth to serve some purpose. Just find the greatest happiness wherever you can and soon you will discover that you have grown up, Aditya. Life is knocking at the door and asking you to wake up. Life has a reason for you too, but at the moment, the first thing to do is to rush to Aprajita. If you love her and she loves you too, then do not be practical. Listen to your heart and do what it tells you to do."

"Uncle D, you really are a great man."

"I know, dude."

"But now you need to show me that you're a great lover which I am not."

"No, Aditya, I'm just a selfish guy, who combined all the reasons – my parents' death, aspirations and my love to come out with the Angel Empire. So that's the short story of the Angel Empire and now just go to your bed as the 'Maggi' is no more eatable (all the water had boiled away and the 'Maggi' had become a pulp.) So goodnight."

I was thinking of her Hitler-like Dad, who was the greatest hurdle and lost in such thoughts, I dozed off.

Next morning, Uncle D kicked my ass, screaming, "Wake up, you lover. It is already 8 o'clock. Get up and rush to her."

"But it is only 8 o'clock."

"So, it is morning. Get up and rush. I wonder how you could sleep all night. I was thinking about you and Aprajita, even after you had gone to sleep. Just go and tell her how much you love her. It is an urgent job that needs to be done."

"In a night-suit?"

"Yes, it is better than being striped. So go and do not bother about anything else."

I left his house while Uncle went and sat on his desk, possibly to check his mail. I was more concerned about Aprajita than his creepy business mails.

He got a mail from friend 09@yahoo.co.in, which was a new and unknown address. He clicked it on and read:

> I am sorry Mr Drishya Roy. I know nothing will change, nor will you feel good after getting this but I am doing it for myself, to make my heart feel better. I know the mistake is not pardonable as I am responsible for spoiling your entire childhood but please try to forgive me if you can. I do not know whether there can be any connection between us, but you are important to me. I am sorry at how foolish I was then.
>
> Rhea

He was completely amazed to receive the mail and replied excitingly.

> Dear Rhea,
>
> There is nothing to apologise for. If today, I, Drishya Roy have achieved the zenith of the corporate world, somewhere down

the line you are responsible for it. The one who falls is capable of getting up and he is the one who best knows how to get up. So thanks to you that I fell and it is because of you that I have got up and become what I am today. One thing for which I want to thank you personally is that you made me realise that love is not merely about sex. Sex is just a stupid game to play, but it has to be played. I have learned what it is like to be with one who is special. It is that which defines love. Love is a feeling which is miles away from the boundaries of sex. It is a feeling that can be felt only from the heart and not by the sex organ. It is a pleasure that gives you the strength to wait for someone throughout your life, to die for someone without waiting for a second. You live for such a person and be yourself as you owe each breath of yours to her. It really drives you crazy, but the madness is about life. You want to live for that someone; you want to make that someone feel proud loving you; you want to prove to that someone how important that person is in your life. That is the spirit of love – to live, to die, to run, to do whatever your heart says just to prove who you are and how important is your life as everyone is in the show to play a role. You did your job which could have been best executed by you only.

Thank you for teaching me all that you did. Had you not taught me the game, my personal situation may have worsened my state.

I do not know what is the link between you and me and where you are at the moment, but one thing is certain, you are another Angel who came from heaven on earth to help me out and please do not feel guilty at all.

One thing I want to let you know is that you taught me that love is not simply about sex. I had not even kissed the girl I loved and still love and neither have I ever wanted to. I just want to love her. Life itself is a most adventurous game and the game we played was an integral part of the big game because deep in my heart, I still respect you Rhea Didi.

Yours lovingly
Drishya (the useless one)

Can I face it all...

Inspired by the great story that I had heard the previous night, I tread on the path leading to her house as it seemed special, although I had been on the same path hundreds of time. That day I was enjoying it all – the rising sun, the calm breeze, the blue sky above my head – everything seemed special and what I enjoyed the most was the fact that I had managed to gather the guts to walk to her house, face her parents and speak out my mind. Maybe this was due to love, which had provoked me to do the job that so far had seemed impossible to me. Now, I had realised that love is really special and my uncle's life story helped boost me to overcome the word 'practical' and cross all the barriers placed by society. I felt special because I had fallen in love. I was the one to know the reason for survival and I was determined to prove to Aprajita that I loved her. She was the one to whom I wanted to prove that I was old enough to move on with the show. I also wanted to let her know that she was the be all and end all of my life. So deeply lost was I in such beautiful thoughts that I did not realise when I had reached my destiny, my love.

I stood outside her house, my hands trembling, my legs shaking, my blood frozen and my mind racing and the only face that came to my mind was that of Hitler (Aprajita's Dad). I imagined that her Dad must have been a much more domineering person than what Aprajita could ever be and without waiting to think more and become weak in my resolve, I managed to press the doorbell. Ding-dong!

'You will soon be a goner, Aditya. If Hitler were to come out, he is sure to kick your ass so hard that it would take years to remove that soreness and you would not be able to walk properly for the rest of your life. I must run away, but if I were to go back, Uncle D would burn my ass. I have nowhere to go except to catch the bull by the horns. Why should I think of Hitler-like Dad or Uncle D? Why could I not think of Aprajita, my love, my *jaanu*? She may come out and open the door to allow me to enter the real world.'

It was the maid who opened the door.

"Is Aprajita home?" I asked very politely.

"Yes! Didi is in her room."

"Can you please tell her that Aditya has come?"

"Yes, just wait."

She left. Oh God, I hoped she would not call the Hitler, because if that happened, my goose was cooked. But she came back after two minutes and opened the gate to say, "Come on inside. Aunty is calling you." (What a crazy maid? When I had told her to call Aprajita, why did she go in and tell her Mom? May be it was funny for her but she had thrown open the gates for greater disasters for me and what with Aprajita's Mom standing at the other end of the garden, gesturing with her hand to enter inside.

"Come in, Aditya," I heard her say.

I was in a fix. She had seen me. Now I could not run back. Moreover Hitler could be waiting inside, sharpening his knife to chop my head. Despite the presence of the bloody butcher and the innocent lamb (me), I could not do anything except to think of the sexy image.

I moved to the living room, trembling in my boots. I knew that if Hitler were to so much as fire at me, nothing was going to work. But I kept on moving in, egged on by Uncle D's words, "Just move on." Finally, I entered the room and the next second I stood rooted to the spot. Hitler sat next to his wife and whispered on looking at me, "Is he the same boy?"

Oh God, he had recognised me! Now he was sure to hang me till death. Oh God, please change my face for a few minutes, I prayed fervently. I knew Aprajita liked my mug but I was sure that she would be more interested in my life than my face. I knew she was much more understanding than her father but of what use was it, caught as I was in such a tight situation?

"Yes! He is the same boy but let him go and see her first," she replied, pointing the stairs to me.

Those words saved me from a certain death. How relieved I was could be seen from my face. Walking like a zombie, I climbed up the staircase, my heart thudding in the ribs.

The final round was round the corner where I had to go straight to Aprajita and declare my love and affection for her. I was ready to drop down on my knees and plead for her love. When I neared the door, I stood as if paralysed at the sight in front of me. She sat with a newspaper in her hand and was crying bitterly. Before I could utter anything, she spoke out, "Aditya, I am sorry about Shahid but I could not stand by your side, because in the same accident, the other person to die was my brother Rahul." Saying this, she burst into tears and began to sob loudly as if the dam of tears had burst.

"What?" I took the newspaper from her hand. It was dated 2nd October, 2009 and read:

> "Bike No.1881 was struck by a drunken truck-driver. The two occupants of the bike were two youngsters who have been identified as Shahid and Rahul Khanna."

"What? Rahul Bhaiya is dead?" I could not believe what had happened. I seemed in a state of confusion and shock and longed to be given a sedative to calm my overworked nerves. I just did not know how to react as I was not prepared for it.

"Why did you not tell me?" I asked her, clutching her arms tightly and shaking her violently. I was about to burst into tears too. I could not control myself from shaking her and shouting at her, "Why? Why?"

She sat rooted to the chair, tears rolling down her cheeks like a stream in flood. After a few minutes, she replied, wiping her tears and my tears simultaneously, "I had rung you up as soon as I came to know of it but your number was switched off (I had broken my phone). I even tried your home number but there was no response (we all were at Shahid's place) and later I learnt that the other person to die in the accident was none other than Shahid. I lost myself completely. I did not want to add to your woes as you already were so disturbed. Arushi knew about it, but I prevented her from telling you and making you worried. That is why I was avoiding you. Had I met you, I would not have been able to hide my emotions."

"How come *Bhaiya* and Shahid were together?"

"On the 1st, after your call, I received a call from *Bhaiya* saying that he was in the city and had bought a cake for the surprise party planned for Mom and Dad. He told me, 'Do not tell anyone but remain awake as I would be reaching home after some time.' Shahid and *Bhaiya* were good friends since their schooldays and Shahid was out on his usual ride and must have offered a lift to *Bhaiya*."

"Why do you care so much for me, Aprajita"? I asked, cupping her face in my hands and trying to wipe her face drenched with tears. What I was surprised at was the fact that how could someone care for me as much as she did and had even forgotten her own loss just to see a smile on my face!

Slapping me lightly on my face, she said, "I love you, *besharam*!"

She has won me over. She was my Aprajita. She loved me a lot and it was time when love had taken over everything, pushing our individual losses to the background. This time none of us bothered about telling how much we loved each other. Our feelings had overtaken our unspoken words in the race to reach our hearts. The four magical letters had really done a great wonder, making me realise how important I was that someone really needed me, that someone cared for me 24 x 7, that there was someone for whom I was prepared to bear and share every kind of pain, that there was someone for whom I really wanted to live and that there was someone who had become special in my life.

I kept on gazing at her and with each passing second, I found her beauty increase. She had taken full possession of my senses. It was so strange that every time I or my heart wanted anything, she would get to know of it beforehand. There was really telepathy at work among us and we were true soulmates – two souls with a common heart. I knew then that nothing could come between us, not even her Hitler-like Dad because she had become my soulmate and I could never lose her. I just wanted her soul inside me and as I could not do that, I pulled her towards me and hugged her so tightly that she started to cry with her head on my shoulder. That was what life was all about, I felt. When someone needs you to cry on your shoulder gives a strange feeling that is completely out of this world. Her tight embrace was the most special moment of my life and I felt important for the first time. My life was complete with her in my arms. Uncle D was right when he said that there would be a girl who would make me feel proud to be a boy and indeed she was, this unbeatable girl.

With her in my arms, I felt time stood still and for the first time in my life God could have heard my voice coming right from the bottom of my heart. There was no need for air to flow, no breaths to be drawn in or expelled out, no voice to hit my eardrums, no thoughts to occupy my brain, no earth below my feet; just the sheer magic of love with our hearts pumping violently was all that we needed. I realised then that love marked just the beginning of the twelve special letters in the word 'relationship', the letters that make love something very special.

With her in my arms, I was completely lost in the fragrance of her body and enjoyed it all for the next fifteen minutes. Suddenly I felt that somebody was staring at us from the window and when I looked up, I noticed that it was her Mom. I quickly released Aprajita and stepped backward. Her Mom came into the room and remarked, "I like you, Aditya."

I felt as if I was floating on cloud nine and left the room in a cheerful mood, thinking that Aprajita was truly indefatigable. The one to die was her real brother and the other was my friend, though I wondered why some relationships were above blood relations!

I had met Aprajita, the one who cannot be beaten by any situation. God must have taken all the time in the world to create a person like her because she was one in many; a girl like her had to be someone special – she, who could be so cunning, so naughty at times, was also so adorable, so affectionate, so caring, so alluring, so cute, so mature, so experienced, so funny and so special too at other times. She had to be a true winner…

I left her house wondering what love was? When you are truly in love, it occupies your mind 24 x 7 and your thoughts start with love and end with the same love each and every moment of your life. The funny thing about love is that you cannot tell why you love someone because love cannot be defined. It is just a feeling, a determination that pushes you to cross all obstacles, be brave and do things that others would not think of even. That was what Aprajita had proved to me.

It was love that had changed the life of Uncle D and he still continued to love his Angel. There was no reason for doing it, considering the fact that Angel had left and got married to someone else, but he had resolved to continue to love her till his death. That is what love is about. Aprajita cared for me a lot and was willing to bear any pain silently for me, without letting me know the pain she was going through because of it. How great she had been!

How could Uncle D be so great to love someone about whom he knew she could never be his? My parents loved me for no reason since my birth and it is said that love is because of the blood relationship but if it were so, then how could Aprajita love me so much when she was not a blood relation? Love has no definition that can be printed in any book (not in mine) or be taught to anyone. It is just a feeling, a trust that is proved over time, particularly in times of adversity when you desperately need someone to hold your hand, to console you and give you strength. I wonder why it was that just a voice was enough to motivate me, to pull me out of the most difficult of situations? It was simply because love had the power to perform great wonders. It was then that I realised that science could never generate a medicine which could push human beings to the deepest depths of love. What is more, when you yourself are in love, you find everyone around to be lost in love. Love can be for studying, for Nature, nation, God, parents, child, sport, art, creation, speed, thrill, adventure, relations; love is for one and all…

Love is a really special feeling and if you are in love, you can feel the four magical alphabets flow in the air. This word, this feeling has existed since creation and is present in each and everything that we see around us – it lies hidden in every face and every creation of God, who Himself was the greatest lover to make us succeed in our love.

Hats off to girls...

Boys are strong and powerful and true winners in the battles of daily life. They tend to forget the tough times easily and live life to the beats of their own music. Boys like me are the ones, who know how to coordinate their body and soul and are the real winners to succeed in life. That is why most of the greatest conquerors were male. But remember, at the end of the day, all men who were conquerors had a Mom and a lover and thus were the real winners, because they knew the meaning of love. Men are considered to be great priests of love but all I remember are my Mom, my sister, my girlfriend, who all have been indefatigable. They all have loved me for no reason and continue to do so even now. I am not anything great to be showered such love but it is their love that has given meaning to my life. I just want to devote my whole life to all of them. They have been the show-stealers, the centres of attraction during all the important phases of my life. They are great and I am lucky to have them in my life. You too just need to open your eyes to look around and you will find that there are always special people, who give your life a meaning, make you feel important and prod you to think about the objective of life. So, live for others and remember, you can make others happy only if you are happy and try to be *aprajita* – the one who cannot be beaten under any circumstances...

Often I have been given to wondering how such a great girl as Aprajita could come to love me because I was nothing great. I have been an ordinary guy, who has been aware of the feeling of love, the immense pleasure that love gives and makes you feel important but I have not been as great a human kind as she has been. The way she has cared for me, loved me and proven her love for me makes me think that no matter how many births I take, I can never be able to beat her. For, after all, she is Aprajita. She is the only one for me…

Live On...........

After settling my issues with Aprajita, I went to see Uncle D who showed me the mail he had received from Rhea (another angel in Uncle D's life). While I was telling him all that had transpired between Aprajita and me, he told me to pen down my life story. So, at the instigation of my uncle and through the will of the Creator in whose hands we all are puppets, I am writing my life story to make my readers know how life can take a turn for the better when you least expect is to do so. Is it not surprising that finally, the story has been compiled...

Today the mass media, including the electronic media, continue to highlight the increase in incidents of live-in relationships, but Uncle D has introduced a new term which he calls 'live-on relationships'. The rise in the trend of live-in relationship has taken a firm foothold on the soil of India. It is a relationship, in which both have a commitment to be with each other because they need each other, but without the need for social recognition. Someone has rightly said, "In India, the society does not permit live-in relationships and therefore, people are forced to marry." If this is so, does this really define love?

Or what Uncle D believes it to be, that is, to live on for the one whom you love, because in love there are no pre-conditions. There is no condition to live together for the rest of one's life. If a couple decides to spend life together cheerfully, there's nothing better than that but if the couple has to face the rusted side of the coin, then that does not mean that the two should cease to live. They have a greater reason to live, to move on and to show how they have loved. Separation teaches us to love and that is why Uncle D has proved his love for Angel, despite being separated from her. The desire to live has taught him to do something extraordinary, something different, something a tad away from this world. All the time he knew that he would never get to marry her, yet he continues to love her to this day and there is no condition like a live-in relationship.

Talking about my love, I feel that Aprajita had dragged our relationship to the verge of collapse as she had told me after Shahid's death that she did not want to live with me but wanted to live only to see a smile on my face. Maybe it was love that had prodded her to say she always wanted to see me happy. She loved me madly and that proved Uncle D's theory in which he describes the live-on relationship as a relationship where one has a relation with life and one lives on just to see the loved one happy (a true human being only can find the reason for living by seeing the happiness of others), so that the chapter of life would end not by seeing a dead face but by seeing millions of smiles. It proves that we should keep moving on to achieve bigger things in life, forget the past and adjust to new situations. That is what life means – to live and to do something to pay the debt you owe for being able to take in every breath of life and by living it to the fullest.

Miss you ANGEL...!

Your face keeps revolving in my mind and I cherish all the moments that we had spent together. I still remember our first meeting when you literally drove me crazy. I am still crazy about you as I love you infinite times more than what I used to when we were together. But we were not destined to be together. I still remember vividly the way it all happened. May be this is called real love because I feel that you are present near me always.

That's why they say love is not what you see, hear, or achieve; it is all that you feel in yourself. You are in love when you touch your heart and feel the touch of that person. I do not know from where your hand comes but I can feel it right over my heart because inside it resides only you. Whenever I close my eyes and recall your face (including the moments spent with you), I take a deep breath and feel your intimacy. I just love the way you do it all – sliding your hand through my hair, kissing my forehead, and I just love not only this, but each and every moment when you are around me.

I have discovered that you are in love not when you think you are in love; you are in love not when you want to be in love; not because of the good looks of a person. In fact you are in love when you keep telling yourself you want to be away from love.

Love is when you die to catch just a glance of that person; love is when you are ready to do anything just to earn a smile from that person; love is when you have tears in your eyes for that person; love is when you start praying for the well-being of that person. That is why I want to announce it loudly, "I LOVE YOU, ANGEL, the love of my life, my *jaan*…I LOVE YOU."

You remember the day when we met (the most special day of my life) and the day we went our separate ways, I thought of you the whole day and that too only about you. I committed the greatest blunder of my life the day when I thought practically; the day when the word 'practical' dragged my feet away from you; the day when I actually realised that I was in love. I went to my place with my eyes full of tears, my heart crying out loudly and mind preoccupied with your forlorn face…

I went and sat in a corner of my room and began to cry. Suddenly a drop struck my face and I closed my eyes. That very moment I saw you in that same white dress, which you were wearing when I saw you and found the love of my life sitting beside me. You took my hand in yours and kissed me in a really special way because for the first time in my life I felt the touch of your lips…

I kept resisting you because each time I got involved with any girl, the scenes of my traumatising past struck my mind. I kept telling you, "No! Baby please, I don't want it. I don't want to be with you. I am a bloody bastard who has spoiled the life of many girls. Please baby, do not do this…"

You simply nodded (the calmness of your face made me lose all my senses). You held my face in your hands (I became numb), you kissed my forehead, slipped your right hand through my hair and left hand on my cheek, before saying in your sweet voice, "*Jaan*, it is not your fault. It had to happen and *mela* baby *to itna* cute *hai, usne to kucch galat kiya hi nahi.*" Baby, it has already been destined by God and we cannot change it. We simply have to accept it and according to me, you had done nothing wrong except to say, "*Mela* baby *to itna* cute *hai*…I love you so much. Just hold my hand so that we can forget everything…"

"No…" I kept resisting but you won. You grabbed my hand tightly and said, "I will make you forget all this, trust me *nah*!"

I simply followed and answered, "Baby trusts you but Baby does not trust himself. He does not want to do something wrong."

"Trust me *nah*!" you persisted and I nodded. Then you said, "I will make you trust yourself."

"Love me, *nah*?"

Again I nodded and you said, "*Bas phir*…tension *kya hai? Kuch nahi*. Just love."

"Kiss me *nah?*"

I nodded but I could not. I did not know how you could take my feelings. You held my face in your hands again and started brushing your lips against mine. The sensation that I felt at that moment cannot be described in words. You kept playing with my lower lip, touching your upper lip with mine at one instant and your lower lip touching my upper lip next. I enjoyed it all and I closed my eyes. There were no other thoughts in my mind. I could feel your breath in my mouth and I loved it all...Then suddenly, I opened my eyes and you disappeared. I do not know why? But I thought, I might be wrong...

I stood up and moved to the other end of the room to look outside the window on the dark night, but I could not locate the moon in the sky. I stood still, looking outside and trying to avoid what was happening between us, because Rhea had left an indelible impression on my mind. Suddenly, you grasped me from behind, turned me hugged me tightly before planting a love bite on my ear. You said, "I will make you forget everything" and then the golden words that you said are still fresh in my mind – "I love you! I love you Baby! I want to be with you forever. I just love you the way you are. I love my *chotta sa, pyaala* baby...I love you *jaan*!" and you kept your head on my shoulder. Staring at you, I found the lost moon in the sky because that day you looked ethereal.

I don't know what made me confess the truth, away from this practical world "I love you too...I love you so much that I do not know myself why I love you." Then came the most memorable moment of my life when we kissed and you really made me forget everything because the only thing in my mind at that time was you; Angel, it was you. The only thing I expected from God was to offer me enough strength to keep you safe and secure in my arms, when suddenly you said, "I want to be in your arms like this forever. I feel so safe and secure."

I turned once to kiss you again and you patted my face, saying, "*Mela ganda baccha.*" You kissed on my nose and again we kissed. You started biting and kissing my neck and we lay down on the floor when you said, "I need a pillow." I offered you my arm and we hugged tightly, lying down on the floor.

My one hand slid through the soft hair of my baby and the other surrounded my baby, sliding to her waist. We lay there in each other's arms as I kept staring at the heaven in front of my eyes. I was in love and wanted to spend my whole life like that, "Thank you *jaan*! You really made me forget everything and now I love my life because you are there. I need to celebrate each and every moment I spend with you. If we are not destined to live together, I just want to keep it all as a beautiful memory in my life."

It was morning by then and the sun's rays struck my closed eyes. When I opened my eyes, I found myself sitting in a corner of my room with wet eyes. You had gone, but you had taught me what I could not teach myself – to forget, to move on and enjoy the auspicious moments of my life. You dragged me out of a world of self-pity, the feeling for which I used to curse myself. I love you, Angel. Angels are messengers of God from heaven to help us...you are my angel, no matter with whom you spend the rest of your life. I will keep you forever in my mind because your Baby wants to be with Angel forever.

Life passed on and you really made me forget my depressing past. Today, I have the name Angel around me all the time because Angel (my Mom, who offered me life, love and who taught me to live) is really special…

If I say I miss you, it is the truth right from my heart because I want you to be with me in each and every moment of my life. When I celebrate, I want you to be with me to share my happiness; when I cry, I need you to hold my hand and hug me tightly and when I am free, I want to talk to you and keep staring at your face. But now I don't have what I need, so during such moments, I close my eyes and revive the memory of my *jaan*, who only can make me complete. Your face comes in front of me and your smile makes the moment complete. But, maybe it would be a lie to say that I do not miss you because there is not a single moment in life when I am able to forget you. You are my *jaan* and I am complete with you always.

Today, Aditya believes that I guided him the right way to love but at the end of the day I know it is my baby, my Angel, who taught me to love, to live and to enjoy. I know that you made my story and we both made Aditya's story.

Remember, you once told me, "Good things happen with good people. It may be late but remember, everyone is good at heart." Yes, it happened as I had hoped for. Today, I received a mail from Rhea and you were right, everyone has been right. Everything was destined and it is just a way of looking at things and I must come back to you….

Missing you…..

Love you……..

Your *jaan*……

Aap ka pyaala Baby…..

Drishya

That's the Life Baby

by Priyesh Ranjan

Price	:	Rs. 125
Pages	:	224
Size	:	5.0 × 7.75 inches
Binding	:	Paperback
Language	:	English
Subject	:	Fiction/Romance
ISBN	:	9788183520003

National Bestseller

About the book:

Sixteen is sweet, Seventeen sweeter and Eighteen is the sweetest!

He thinks so.

What about Love at Eighteen? It happens, everyday! Doesn't it?

True for him!

Have a lot of girls in your life. It feels macho to have options. Girls don't need the advice. They are the wiser sex and have been playing multi-boying games for eons.

.....*But he has three gorgeous damsels, all envious and shooting high testosterone levels.*

How will you thank god if your balcony faces a girls' hostel? .....By being there 24X7? May be!

Exactly what he aims at!

Skirts lead to scandals. Don't they? Ban it or allow scandals.

He loves both, skirts and scandals.

What does he think about 'committed' tag?

You can't keep on eating the same chocolate all the time! Feels like jailed!!!

Meet Abhi. He is one of you with a devil's head! A year at Kota and his life remains no more the same. It all starts with a Bollywood-style love at first sight with Aditi. He sees, he falls, he cajoles and a little luck makes them one! Together they write new rules of dating & romance. Their amorous adventures will make you feel the passion of adolescence. But one day everything changes. How? What? Why? Answers lie in the story.

A stormy honeymoon of emotions......Get ready to laugh and cry!!!

Let's Get Committed...

by Smita & Utkarsh

Price	:	Rs. 125
Pages	:	240
Size	:	5.0 × 7.75 inches
Binding	:	Paperback
Language	:	English
Subject	:	Fiction/Romance
ISBN	:	9788183520157

About the book:

Hierarchy of modern age love:

Orkut > Chatting > Phone > CCD > Movies

Apurv and Radhika get committed. They try to adjust to their new marital status committed by proving the equation 1+1=1.

~ Facebook status = In a relationship…Orkut status: committed.

~ In a given area, low population density implies hands together & lesser, lips and cheeks.

~ 1st testimonial from him/her…scrapbook full of sweetheart/love.

~ Desktop wallpaper = "C:\my pictures\my.sweetheart.jpg"

This stage relates to the fact that even after liking each other, they just experiment with the concept of being together and not because of love…just in hope that they might (if it's written) fall in it.

Being a hottie, Radhika initially misses the single tag and the direct and indirect benefits associated with it. Apurv tries to reinstate the feeling of love in her but fails…though partially…

Life goes on as time tests their compatibility and then suddenly destiny shows its darker side…

Radhika is gone…

What happens next….

If it's love, will it cease to exist if they are apart?

Does Apurv find a new love?